# KILLER NOTE

STELLA KNOX SERIES: BOOK SIX

MARY STONE
STACY O'HARE

Copyright © 2022 by Mary Stone

All rights reserved.

No part of this book may be reproduced in any form or by any electronic or mechanical means, including information storage and retrieval systems, without written permission from the author, except for the use of brief quotations in a book review.

❦ Created with Vellum

# DESCRIPTION

**One wrong note can lead to murder.**

FBI Special Agent Stella Knox's search for her father's murderer is put on hold when three bodies are discovered seated in a wealthy Tennessee suburb. It's strange. The victims seem to be placed in front of a grand piano like an unwilling audience. Stranger still, the killer stopped to eat, taking the plates and silverware with them.

And that's just the beginning.

When security footage reveals the murderer wore a terrifying rabbit mask, Stella and her team know they're dealing with their most unpredictable killer yet. They need to crack the case fast, or the bunny's kill rate will multiple.

It does.

When two more victims are found similarly arranged and garroted with a piano wire, it's clear the unsub is escalating and with no signs of stopping. Time is running out for Stella and the team to solve the case...before another victim's untimely finale.

*Baffling and eerie, Killer Note is the sixth book in the Stella Knox series by bestselling author Mary Stone and Stacy O'Hare that will make you reconsider ever falling asleep to music again.*

# 1

Jeremy Deem rested his head against the back of the chair. Despite his intentions to remain still and unresponsive, he swayed with the cadence of the *allegro maestoso*.

His Steinway grand had never sounded so good. The warm timbre of the notes resonated against the walls. This was what his instrument had been created for.

Chopin. The composer's Piano Concerto no. 1, with all its unusual modulations, was so beautiful Jeremy could almost ignore the fact that he was tied to a chair.

Almost.

*Focus!*

He'd been warned of serious consequences if he allowed his attention to stray from the concert that had been forced upon him.

To shift his mind away from the rope cutting off his circulation, Jeremy studied the music and the musician. If he were to criticize the playing, Jeremy might say the pianist was more precise than passionate, more technical than touched. This movement was an *allegro* not a *presto*.

*The tempo is there, but where's the joy? Where's the heart?*

Not that Jeremy had any right to criticize. The playing was far more accomplished than anything his own clumsy plink-plonking could have achieved. And yet, something was off. The music missed affection. There was no *feeling*, no understanding of the composer's emotional journey. For all the pianist's shoulder jerks and frantic key bashing, the playing was cold and distant.

Dull.

The pianist bent over the Steinway, seemingly oblivious of his "captive" audience. His long fingers plucked at the black and white keys. The performer's morning suit was old-fashioned, a pastiche of how musicians were supposed to dress for performances. The long sleeves of his dinner jacket were scrunched almost to his elbows. His lusterless shoes, probably once polished to a high sheen, pumped at the pedals.

Jeremy imagined the pianist's expression would be the definition of concentration, but he couldn't see the player's face.

Only the rabbit mask.

The large costume piece had seen better days. The pink material inside the long, erect ears was faded. Two of the whiskers were missing from the left side of the rabbit's nose, while a whisker on the right was bent and folded, appearing less like an animal's sensors and more like a bolt of lightning exploding out of a nostril.

Unwilling to study the mask any longer, Jeremy's attention drifted from the musician to the summer sunset framed in the living room's full-length windows. Wispy clouds darkened into shades of pink, purple, and crimson, a beautiful contrast to his estate's green lawn.

The shifting colors helped. Watching the sunset, ignoring his immediate surroundings, Jeremy might have even enjoyed the performance, if he could only move his arms or stretch his legs.

Or call for help.

But he could do none of those things. He was bound tightly to one of his own dining room chairs. His wife sat next to him. Penny's dark brown eyes were open wide and as serious as he'd ever seen them. Penny didn't often worry. All the lines around her eyes were from smiling. Everything about Penny was simple, including her comfortable clothes. Witnessing her fear and confusion softened his heart.

Now, the woman on the other side of Penny? That hardened his heart back up.

Where his wife was soft and tender like a newborn lamb, his mother-in-law was about as flexible as an iron ax. Margaret's steel-gray hair, cut close and curly against her scalp, wouldn't budge in a hurricane.

Nor would she. Jeremy had tied them himself, using the rope the pianist had supplied. With a gun aimed at the back of his head, he'd been forced to do the job well.

When he was done, when he'd pulled the knot tight and gazed into his wife's teary eyes, Jeremy sank into the last seat. He'd trembled as the pianist wound the coarse, scratchy rope around his chest, securing his arms to his sides.

His numb, throbbing fingers kept distracting him from the music. The gun that had been pressed into the base of his skull sat atop the black grand piano. Just the sight of it marred the instrument's pristine surface. A pair of tattered white gloves, the fingertips worn and gray, lay next to the gun.

All of it was distracting, but the pianist's appearance threw this *stranger-than-fiction* scenario into uncharted territory.

Jeremy didn't understand how he could see anything

through the giant rabbit head. Of all the masks this madman could've chosen...

*What's happening?*

*And why us?*

Jeremy cursed himself for the hundredth time for not being more vigilant before opening his front door. But why would he? They'd been expecting his son and granddaughter. When he'd heard a knock and swung the door open with excitement about an hour ago, the sight of the rabbit's face was so unexpected, so shocking, he hadn't even noticed the gun dangling from a gloved hand.

Fear ate at his sanity as worry for Jem and little Ellie caused a fresh wave of panic.

*Where are they?*

Had they been delayed, or had the rabbit delayed them? Were they also tied up right now somewhere else? Or worse?

As worry hummed through Jeremy's system, the pianist played on, moving from the *allegro maestoso* to the *romanze* movement. Chopin himself wrote that the *romanze* should call forth a thousand happy memories. Instead, that movement would be the soundtrack of his nightmares for the rest of Jeremy Deem's life.

If he had a life left once the bunny took his leave.

The pianist thumped out the last chords and raised his right arm from the instrument, hand aloft in triumph.

Jeremy would have applauded if he'd been able. Chopin's Piano Concerto no. 1 wasn't an easy piece, and Jeremy had detected no mistakes. This performer's technical skills were quite impeccable.

Maybe if they applauded loudly enough, this rabbit-faced intruder would decide he'd had enough and leave them alone. But Jeremy could barely wriggle his fingers.

"Wonderful, wonderful," he choked through a mouth so dry it could barely form the words. "Well done. Bravo."

"Yes, yes. Very...very good." Though her voice was reedy and thin, Penny did her best to help.

Jeremy glanced at her from the corner of his eye.

*Come on, hun. You can do better.*

His wife so often depended on him for guidance. She usually waited for him to express an opinion before daring to say anything herself, and then she'd only speak in agreement. Jeremy shouldn't have to tell her—in this stressed-out, intense moment—to be more passionate in her praise. He raised his volume, hoping to encourage her to do the same.

Anything to get this lunatic out of their house.

"*Bravo!*"

The rabbit lowered his arm. He shifted in his seat, facing his captive audience. "Why, thank you. You're too kind. Far too kind."

"That's for sure." Margaret spat the words like darts at a target.

Penny's mother was never one to hide her feelings or apply praise when it wasn't deserved.

Or even when it was.

"Shut up," Jeremy hissed. "She doesn't mean that—"

"I mean every word." It sounded like she was gargling gravel. "Worst rendition of Chopin I've heard in more than half a century. You're all fingers and no feeling. Like listening to a music box. Now, if you're done murdering a masterpiece, it's time to leave. Go on, you loon. Get out."

"Mom! Please." Penny's eyes were flooded with terror.

Margaret ignored her daughter. It wasn't the first time she'd neglected to listen to her child—and Jeremy hoped it wouldn't be the last. "I'm not scared of this idiot. I'm eighty-six years old. There's nothing this fool can do to me that nature and bad luck haven't already done." She jutted her chin toward the front door. "Now, go on. Get. You fat-fingered lunatic."

Penny trembled so badly the legs of the chair rattled on the parquet floor. "Mommy, no! Please."

The pianist's silence was more disturbing than any alternative reaction he could've had. Slowly, delicately, he lifted one white glove and slid it over the long, pale fingers of his right hand.

Jeremy held his breath.

"That's perfectly fine, Mrs. Taylor." His voice was high and restrained, though muffled through the rabbit mask, making the words sound distant, like a child speaking from under a blanket. "If one can't take criticism, one shouldn't pursue the arts. I shall take a short break now. I'll return in short order."

The pianist removed a phone from the inner pocket of his jacket and placed it on the stool beside him. When he touched the screen, Rachmaninoff's Piano Concerto no. 3 sounded through the device's tinny speaker.

"You may enjoy this little recording while I take my break." His right hand then strayed to the top of the piano, moving to where the pistol rested. He lifted the gun, turned, and aimed it at Margaret. The weapon seemed impossibly large, the muzzle darker than a starless sky. "Whoever falls asleep gets their brains blown out."

The pianist pulled on his other glove and crossed to the French doors at the end of the living room. With both hands, he threw the glass doors that led to the dining room open, leaving his arms extended as though accepting the applause of a thousand fans.

Margaret looked ready to follow the rabbit into the dining room, chair and all. "Bastard."

"Mother, stop." Penny's voice had taken on a whiney edge. "But doesn't he seem familiar? Something about the way he plays…"

"He plays like a sloth."

"Shhh!"

The bound trio fell silent.

Jeremy gritted his teeth, letting his frustration show now that the intruder wasn't staring straight at him.

This was *his* house. Jeremy had paid over fifteen million dollars for this estate. For that kind of money, his security systems should have kept this crazed musician or kidnapper or whatever he was *out*. But there the madman was, walking around freely like he owned the place.

*And I let him in.*

The pianist strode through the double doors into the dining room.

Until a couple of years ago, that room had rarely been used. Before Margaret moved in, he and Penny were content to eat their meals on the island in the kitchen. If he worked late, or was out meeting a client, Penny would eat alone on the sofa, a tray on her lap, a rerun of *Law and Order* on the television.

Since Penny's mother came to live with them, she'd insisted evening meals be eaten in the formal dining room. Food was served on their best china, brought to the table under polished silver cloches, and eaten beneath the stormy clouds of Albert Bierstadt's *Buffalo Trail*. The nineteenth-century western landscape threw a dark pall over the family dinner.

At least Jeremy had kept his place at the head of the table, consigning Margaret to the seat next to him. This was his house, dammit. But, apparently, mothers-in-law and rabbit-faced criminals didn't understand how home ownership worked.

Earlier tonight, the trio had been sitting at the table, unrolling their napkins, when the doorbell rang. The table was still set with meals they'd barely touched. The cloches had most likely created sweat rings that would need to be buffed out of the wood.

Penny had sprung to her feet as the bell echoed through the house, her eyes wide with anxiety. "They're early. I wasn't expecting them for dinner."

Jeremy had waved her down, promising to order takeout if needed. "It'll be fine, dear."

It hadn't been their son and granddaughter on the porch when Jeremy opened the door, though. And it wasn't fine. Not at all.

Hatred boiled through Jeremy's veins as he watched the pianist take his seat at the dining table. He laid the gun on the table and lifted the cloche. The smell of salmon and asparagus, of butter sauce and parsley, drifted Jeremy's way on the breeze from the air conditioner.

Jeremy pulled at the ropes.

The pianist slid up the bottom of his mask, revealing a smooth chin and narrow, thin lips. He took up the silver knife and fork. With delicate movements, he cut into the salmon and chewed, his head swaying with the concerto playing on his phone.

*That's my dinner, dammit!*

"I hope you choke on it, you—"

*Bang.*

Penny screamed as a bullet whistled past Jeremy's face and embedded itself into the Darwin Rhodell original hanging above the sectional in the living room. The side of the frame cracked, pulling a strip of snakeskin, representing the outline of the sunset, loose. The painting was worth twenty thousand dollars—an eighty percent jump in valuation since the artist had been arrested for multiple murders.

"You shoot like you play," Margaret shouted. "With hands like those, I'm glad you didn't do my hip replacement. You'd have taken out my ovaries."

"Mom, please!"

"Shh." The pianist set the gun back on the table. "Listen to the music. Or the next shot will go through someone's ear." He helped himself to another piece of salmon.

Jeremy breathed out slowly, trying to calm his pounding heart. If he'd bought a smaller house with less extensive grounds, maybe someone would have heard that shot and be calling the police. But he'd picked this place specifically for the seclusion granted by the long private drive and five acres of land. They were entirely alone.

The pianist finished his meal and wiped his mouth on the napkin. Then he rolled the cutlery back into the creamy-white cloth napkin and set them on the plate. Readjusting his mask, he stood.

He picked up the gun and returned through the French doors to the music room. In one smooth motion, the rabbit lifted the phone, stopped the music, and slipped it back into his pocket. "How are we all doing? No one's fallen asleep, I hope."

Pacing, the rabbit stopped in front of Jeremy. Somewhere behind the creature's oversized black eyes were the pianist's eyes. But even as the bewhiskered mask crept closer until they were nose to nose, Jeremy couldn't see through any part of it.

The rabbit shook his head. "No, you're awake."

He moved on to Penny. "And you're wide awake. Good, good."

Penny nodded vigorously. "Yes, yes. I'm not sleeping. I'll never sleep again. I swear to God."

The rabbit stopped in front of Margaret. "And you haven't—"

"No, I haven't fallen asleep, you idiot. You think I'd miss this? Watching a giant rabbit eat my son-in-law's below-average dinner was the most fun I've had in years."

The rabbit straightened. "Good. Then you'll live to hear another piece."

"Wasn't *that* much fun," Margaret muttered.

The pianist flicked out the tail of his morning coat before sinking back onto the stool. He set down the gun and peeled off his gloves. For a moment, he sat there, fingers flexed. Jeremy wondered what he was waiting for. Then, without warning, he launched into the opening movement of Saint-Saëns's Piano Concerto op. 44 no. 4 in C Minor.

Jeremy raised his eyebrows. As much as he hated the lunatic in the fancy pants, he respected his technical expertise. Saint-Saëns's piece wasn't played often and for good reason. Without the right care and emotional input, the tune could come across as simple and uninteresting.

A few bars into the piece, however, Jeremy discovered a problem.

The rabbit's care and emotional input were sorely lacking.

All Jeremy heard was a flow of notes with little to connect them. Several minutes in, it was everything he could do to keep from yawning. He leaned back against the chair. The piece was close to half an hour long. Maybe they'd be set free after that.

The house was full of valuables. Jewelry. Cash. Heck, there was about five hundred thousand dollars' worth of watches in a drawer in his walk-in closet alone. Jeremy would joyfully slip every one of them onto the rabbit's wrists if he would just leave.

But the freak remained, playing one obscure piano concerto after another with emotionless precision.

This went on for hours.

Liszt, Ravel, Bach, Beethoven, back to Ravel. Every classical composer who'd ever written a piece for a piano came from Jeremy Deem's piano.

The hands on the carriage clock at the end of the room ticked on. Midnight. One. Two. Still the music came, one concerto after another. Half the night they'd been sitting there, strapped in place, and still, the playing continued.

Next to Jeremy, Penny shifted in her seat. His wife couldn't normally sit still. Even when they took a private jet to Europe, she'd spend twenty minutes of every hour on her feet.

*She must be in agony.*

Finally, the rabbit banged out the last note of an *allegro* and lifted his hands in the air.

"Marvelous." Jeremy spoke but was unable to summon any enthusiasm. His hands and feet were numb. His jaw ached from keeping his face on the pleasant side of neutral. "You play magnificently. Now, please. Just go."

"Still awake then? Why, yes, you are. Wonderful. Such a polite audience. But I couldn't possibly abandon you now. How about a little Rachmaninoff?"

Margaret sighed deeply. "How about you Rachmaninoff outta here? It's past my bedtime." She shifted as much as her bindings would allow. "I need to pee."

*Margaret. Direct as always.*

"Hold it."

"I can't. When you get to my age, you won't be able to either."

"Then don't hold it." The pianist cracked his fingers. "I don't care."

"You son of—"

Rachmaninoff's Romance in A Minor drowned out the elderly woman's rant.

Jeremy sighed. It was little more than juvenilia. Without the violin accompaniment, the piano sounded lost and alone, but the pianist didn't seem to care. He played on, returning to Chopin without a break, then murdering Liszt's Piano

Sonata in B Minor before shifting to Vivaldi, as though he were playing in the finals of the International Johann Sebastian Bach Competition and wanted to show the judges the breadth of his abilities.

He played on, insulting Grieg, then bashing Shostakovich until they were in their eighth hour without moving.

Jeremy rolled his neck. He had to do something. "Mister, why don't you—?"

The pianist's fingers didn't slow. "I'll be done when I say I'm done. And not before. And remember, no sleeping. Or you die."

He played on.

*How much longer can this lunatic go on? Surely he can't know many more pieces.*

But the rabbit seemed to be an encyclopedia of music.

Jeremy closed his eyes but remembered the warning and snapped them open. The carriage clock chimed. Two thirty. A loud snore rumbled from Margaret's chair.

The playing stopped instantly. The pianist's fingers hung frozen over the keyboard.

For the first time in hours, since he'd eaten Jeremy's dinner, the house was absent of music.

The air-conditioning unit hummed. The clock ticked. And Margaret snored.

Slowly, the pianist swiveled on his stool. He pulled on his gloves again, one at a time.

Jeremy lowered his head, hoping a display of respect might serve them well. "Please, whatever you want, just take—"

*Bang.*

Jeremy's head jerked up as Penny's scream drowned out the bullet's echo. The gun smoked in the rabbit's hand.

Margaret's head rolled back.

For a moment, Jeremy thought his mother-in-law was

still sleeping. Her chin was pointed up, with the top of the chair serving as a headrest.

But blood dripped from the back of her skull, landing with soft plops on the wooden floor.

"Mommy!"

*Bang.*

Penny's face swiveled toward Jeremy. Dark red blood inched across her forehead, oozing in a thick line from the hole above her eyebrow to the bridge of her nose and into her eye. It turned pink as it mixed with a river of tears and continued down her face.

Jeremy watched her kind, gentle light fade away.

"No. Penny. No!" Jeremy tried to shove the chair back, pushing himself out of reach. "No, no. Please, no."

The rabbit lowered the gun. He slipped the weapon into the pocket of his morning coat. "Don't worry. I won't shoot you."

Jeremy couldn't focus on anything except his wife. Her eyes were still so wide. He waited for her to blink, but she'd never blink again.

*Penny. Oh, Penny.*

The rabbit reached into his other pocket and pulled out a short coil of piano wire. "I've got something special for you, sleepyhead."

## 2

*It's another weird one.*

FBI Special Agent Stella Knox contemplated her boss's words as she rested her gloved hands on her hips and studied the crime scene she'd been called to less than an hour ago.

She'd gone from enjoying a free Sunday of brunching and visiting friends to yet another murder, this one in the upscale Nashville suburb of Kentwood.

Standing in the spacious home of one Jeremy Deem, she was dressed from head to toe in Tyvek, examining three dead bodies. The cloying, coppery smell of dried blood permeated her N90 mask.

The hood on her white forensic suit bulged over her dark ponytail, pulling the elastic tight against the top of her forehead. She sighed.

A part of her hated wearing the suits, but a bigger part understood why the wise local medical examiner had implemented the policy. Sure, the gear protected humans, but more than that, it protected crime scenes from human error. It saved the crime scene unit time and resources by reducing the need to separate trace evidence that belonged to the scene from evidence brought in by the team.

Still, the red line above her eyebrows would last for hours.

*Better than a bullet to the skull, so quit complaining and do your job.*

Sufficiently self-scolded, Stella cast a critical gaze at her surroundings.

To her right, a forensic tech ran a brush over the keys of a piano that probably cost more than she made annually. As she watched, the tech shook his head.

"Nothing?" she asked.

"It's been wiped, but I'll check every inch."

She shot him a thumbs-up and turned her attention to another tech examining a painting that appeared to have taken a bullet to the canvas.

Stella shuddered as she studied the artwork. A Darwin Rhodell. She'd recognize those broad, colorful strokes with Rhodell's "creative" add-ons in her sleep. A strip of snakeskin dangled free from the canvas. His art had initially included nature elements—tree bark, flower petals. At some point, he'd escalated to animal pieces like fur and snakeskin. Finally, he'd included human parts.

For all the supposed beauty in Rhodell's art, the only things Stella saw were dismembered corpses, a bleeding colleague, and the gallery basement where he'd held her and another young woman captive. Somehow, those events had driven up the price of his work. If anything, it seemed strangely appropriate that Rhodell's art would be at the scene of another horrific crime.

"Did you find the bullet?"

The tech held up an evidence bag. "Got a single 9mm."

Terrific. A 9mm bullet single was the most popular handgun cartridge in the world. That little bit of knowledge wouldn't help them narrow down the type of gun used to shoot it.

A flash made her blink. She turned. The forensic photographer snapped two pictures of the piano stool before shifting focus to three dark fragments of brain matter drying on the floor.

Stella stayed out of the way as the photographer worked. He would need to take a lot of pictures in this room. Everything about it was wrong.

Three chairs were arranged in a line, facing the piano. These were the unsub's audience members, Stella theorized. Front-row seats, giving him...or her...their full attention.

Two victims, both women, had received a single bullet to the brain. The way they rested—the older woman with her head rolled back and the younger woman with hers turned to the side—they could have been sleeping. Only the blood streaked across their faces and the sticky red puddles beneath the chairs showed they would never wake from this nightmare.

The third victim, a man who appeared to be in his early sixties, had suffered a much more painful death.

The medical examiner would provide definitive answers. But judging by the deep red line around the man's neck, his blood-soaked collar, and the way his eyes bulged out of his blue-gray face, he'd been garroted.

"It's weird, right?" Special Agent Ander Bennett's deep, confident voice sounded muffled as he came up behind Stella.

Even with white coveralls covering his blond curls and his face hidden behind a mask, Stella recognized her colleague's large frame. He was a tall man with broad shoulders. His strong chin and easy smile got him free desserts and winks from waitresses. And, sometimes, a phone number on the back of the receipt. Stella had seen that in action a handful of times.

"Not a normal Sunday, that's for sure. You just get here?"

"About two minutes ago. Slade is in the garden with the local police chief, and the others are on the way. Except for Mac and Dani, of course."

Stella took a deep breath and pressed a hand to her stomach at the mention of her friends and colleagues. "Of course."

An hour ago, she'd had the entire day planned out. After sleeping late, she was going to enjoy a leisurely brunch at the little café below her apartment. Once her tank was filled, she'd visit Special Agents Mackenzie Drake and Danielle Jameson to see if they were better or worse than when she'd left them at three that morning.

She still couldn't believe it.

Dani and Mac had been abducted during their last case and tortured for several hours before Stella and the team managed to find and free them. Mac had been held in a crate and waterboarded, and that was after she'd survived a car wreck. She would need some time to recover, mentally and physically.

Dani, at eight months pregnant, had survived the same car wreck and fought hand-to-hand combat with the perpetrator. She was heading straight into maternity leave now. She wouldn't be back for a while. Stella hoped that holding her baby and staring into the face of the future would help the past fade away faster.

Ander stepped toward the dead trio and crossed his arms over his chest. "What do you make of this?"

Chewing her bottom lip, Stella considered her initial impression of the scene. "I get the two shootings. But if you're going to torture someone, I'd expect to see additional abuse on the male victim."

"Abuse? You think he was tortured? For what? To talk?"

"That was my initial impression up until I got closer. Now..." She shook her head.

Ander came around and stood next to her, taking in the victims. He rocked on his heels. "I see your thinking. Killer asks for the combination to the safe. Victim tells him to get lost. Killer pops one of the captives to show he means business, but the victim still doesn't hand over the combination. Killer pops the other one and still, the victim says nothing. So the killer garrotes him?"

Stella bent forward. Resting her hands on her knees, she examined the man. He still had all his fingers and fingernails. There were no cuts on his face or burn marks on his neck. Even his thin, gray hair was barely out of place.

"Doesn't work, though, does it? He's not going to say much with a cut larynx."

"Maybe he talked before he was garroted?"

Stella straightened. Apart from the three chairs, the victims, the damaged painting, and the blood-splattered floor, nothing else in the room appeared out of place. The overpriced, overstuffed sofa on the other side of the room was undisturbed. The sheepskin rug was unblemished. Even the glass cabinet was unscratched, its carriage clock and antique ivory carvings in showroom condition.

"I don't know. I'd expect to see more damage here, you know? Drawers open. Stuff smashed. It's like the killer didn't even bother searching for anything before he moved on to shooting people. And why do it in front of the piano? It's all too...clean."

"That reminds me. Check this out."

Ander headed toward an open pair of double doors. Stella followed him into a large dining room dominated by an exquisite table long enough to seat twelve. Three chairs were missing from the foot of the table. At the head, three places had been laid.

He stood at the foot of the table and gestured to the empty spaces. "Looks like he took the chairs from here."

Stella frowned. The elastic in her hood slid up against her forehead. Irritated, she pushed it back into place. "He could have killed them all here if he'd wanted to. But he took them over to the piano before he did the deed."

Ander headed toward the other end of the table. "Maybe if he'd killed them here, it would have ruined his dinner. Check it out."

Stella joined him at the head of the table. On two of the three places, a silver dome rested next to polished cutlery and a white cloth napkin, revealing a plate with only a few bites missing. The third setting contained only a placemat. The silver dome stood to one side, the plate, napkin, and silverware missing.

She lifted a hand to her ear. Her gloved fingers didn't find the gold stud her father had given her as a teenager, but the scrunchy material of the forensic hood. She dropped her hand. Stella couldn't wait to take that suit off. "Has forensics gone through this yet?"

Ander nodded. "Preliminarily. I already asked. Salmon and asparagus in what looks like butter and parsley sauce. Might have been nice once. Kinda congealed now. They don't recommend it."

Stella's hand drifted toward her ear again. She reversed course and set her hands on her hips. "If the meal was cooked last night and they were killed before they could eat very much, that should help us with a timeline. It's coming up on midday now, so not more than seventeen, eighteen hours ago."

Ander leaned over the dining room table, examining the setup. "Right. But why only two place settings?"

"The killer stopped to eat. Took the plates and silverware with him."

Ander's eyebrows shot toward his curly hairline, now smushed down by his suit's hood. "How do you know?"

Stella held a latex-clad finger above the side of a silver dome. A gray crescent as light as a salt stain decorated the table next to its edge. "See the residue? That's a water stain, the reason you put coasters on your coffee table. The dome caught the steam from the food and condensed, then, *voila*, water stain."

"You put coasters on your coffee table? Hagen would be impressed."

Stella laughed. Hagen's fastidiousness and her own style didn't really mesh. "Not me. But people like Hagen who have nice things normally do."

Nice was an understatement when it came to the Deems' possessions. The expensive-looking dining table was next level. Even the chairs gleamed. No dust lingered on frames or sideboards. Back in the music area, the piano's black body shined like a polished mirror.

Ander's breath rasped against the inside of his mask. "You think the killer popped his victims then sat down and tucked into one of their dinners? Then he took a knife, fork, spoon, and plate with him to make sure he didn't leave any DNA? That's cold."

"Or he killed one and took a dinner break before he got back to work. Or he ate and then killed. Nothing's certain, but I think it's a pretty good guess the salmon and asparagus are now in the belly of our killer."

"Like I said, cold."

Stella leaned closer to the silver dome on one of the plates. Her reflection, with its white hood, stretched out before her. She looked like a scientist on an alien planet. "However he did it, he thought this thing through. There aren't too many killers who take their dishes. Weirdly enough, plenty who eat. Apparently, killing triggers a healthy appetite."

Beyond her own reflection in the cloche, two more Tyvek-clad figures entered the crime scene. The rustle of material sounded incongruous in front of the polished grand piano, as though someone had blown their nose in the middle of a performance.

The smaller of the new arrivals lifted a gloved hand in greeting. Special Agent Chloe Foster was unmistakable. Her normally all-black ensemble was covered in white. At five-four, she was a couple of inches shorter than Stella. But the way she squared her hips and shoulders as she walked was reminiscent of a pit bull and made her appear taller. Especially now that her arm was no longer in a sling.

She'd been injured a few weeks ago, but Chloe Foster wasn't one to let a little bullet keep her from the job.

Chloe stopped short in front of the damaged Rhodell painting. For a moment, she stood there, staring at the image, now crooked and destroyed. "Someone shoulda shot this thing twice."

"Maybe three or four times." Hagen Yates was almost as tall as Ander, slimmer but equally toned. As he strode toward the dining room, his dark green eyes passed from Ander, who he greeted with a short nod, to Stella, where his attention remained.

Supervisory Special Agent Slade's call hadn't been the first she'd received that day.

As Stella had been in the process of tucking into her brunch, Hagen's name had appeared on her screen. He'd seemed nervous, almost agitated when he'd said he needed to tell her about something. Stella wasn't sure exactly what that something was—Slade's call had interrupted them—but she was certain it concerned her father. And probably his too.

Both their fathers had been murdered. Stella's dad, a Memphis cop, was killed in the line of duty when Stella was fourteen.

Hagen's dad had been a defense lawyer, killed on the courthouse steps by the kinds of people her dad usually arrested.

Now Hagen was helping Stella find the dirty cops who'd killed her father. They'd already found her dad's former partner. Despite allegedly being killed over a decade back, he was alive and well, living in Atlanta under witness protection.

Stella appreciated the help she'd gotten so far in her investigation. But exactly why Hagen was helping her, she wasn't sure. She didn't know whether his motivation was professional or personal in that he saw her as an avenue to answers. And, until she knew, she couldn't entirely trust him, not outside the job anyway.

They needed to talk. But that talk would have to wait.

"Everyone here?"

SSA Slade stepped into the dining room behind her.

Alongside him was a second figure, a woman. The temples of her wide-framed glasses were tucked into the hood of her forensic suit, but otherwise, Stella couldn't get a good grasp on her features. She shifted uncomfortably. The Tyvek on her arms rubbed noisily against her hips.

"This is Chief Jean Gray. She's in charge of law enforcement in Kentwood. She's been filling me in on the victims here."

Chief Gray lifted a hand in greeting but said nothing.

Ander greeted Slade and the chief with a slight nod. "Boss, are Caleb and Martin on this case?"

"Nope. Martin's still assisting on that drug case while Caleb's tied up on the bank fraud. I might be able to call them in for limited assistance. With Mac and Dani out, we're officially two down. Without Martin and Caleb, that takes it to four down. So you'll have to work twice as hard."

Chloe shifted, and her suit made a rude noise. "Great. If we add a couple of hours to the day and a couple of days to the week, we should be fine."

Slade ignored Chloe's complaint. "As you can see, we've got three victims. The male is Jeremy Deem. He owns a finance company."

"That explains the twenty-thousand-dollar criminal artwork, I guess."

Slade ignored Chloe yet again. "The other two victims are his wife, Penny, and her mother, Margaret. They were found this morning by the housekeeper, Candice Diaz. Forensics is packing up the computers and phones, but nothing appears to have been taken. Chief Gray, however, has a lead. Chief?"

Chief Gray blinked twice, her overly mascaraed eyelashes sweeping the lenses of her glasses. "Hm?"

Stella couldn't tell if the chief was having a hard time hearing because of the suit hood or if she wasn't paying attention. Maybe she was in shock?

"The footage?" Slade prompted.

"The...oh. Yes. Of course." She pulled a phone out of the pocket of her coveralls and ran a finger over the screen. Nothing happened. "Oh, damn these things. Never did like them." She peeled off one glove and dropped it onto the table. Stella swiped it up, not wanting anything but evidence on the surface. Chief Gray didn't appear to notice. She brought her phone screen to life and opened the video player. "This is from the security company. It's the camera above the front door."

She set the phone on the table. Stella picked that up as well, and the others gathered around her.

The front porch stretched across each side of the screen,

the wide-angle lens bending the pillars until they resembled the ribs of a whale.

A figure approached the door, tote bag slung over an arm.

At first, it seemed like a tall shadow with a head stretching longer than humanly possible. Then the figure stepped into the light.

Stella jolted at the sight of a giant rabbit head staring into the camera. The eyes were huge black holes. Long ears wobbled in the evening breeze. A buck-toothed half-grin smiled eerily. There were even whiskers and bits of fur.

For a moment, Stella couldn't quite sort out what she was seeing. Dark clothing, definitely. Black shoes were scuffed to the point of almost appearing gray. Black pants stretched beneath a morning coat with a tail reaching down the back of the figure's thighs. All of that was normal enough.

Then there were the pale elements. A white shirt looked a bit worn. White gloves poked out beneath the black jacket sleeves.

Chloe asked the million-dollar question. "What the hell is that?"

"A rabbit?" Stella barely heard herself answer as she watched the strangeness unfold.

The rabbit rang the doorbell.

As the visitor waited, he reached one gloved hand into the jacket's right pocket.

The door opened, and the rabbit pulled out a gun. Instead of pointing it at the person still off camera, he held the weapon loosely by his side. He must have said something, but the video had no sound. Then he passed under the camera, one rabbit ear tip brushing the lens, before he disappeared into the house.

Chloe blew out a breath. The release rasped through her mask. "The lineup will be tricky. We're going to need a fox, a chicken, a dog, and a cat."

"Right." Ander's laugh seemed strained. "Maybe Bugs—"

Slade held up a hand. "No Bugs Bunny or Roger Rabbit comments, please."

Ander's teeth clicked shut.

Stella shook her head, trying to process the chain of events. "Why did they even answer the door? They've got security cameras." Stella waved at the proof in her hand.

"Once we have someone to interview, we can hopefully answer that. At the moment, this freak is all we've got." As Stella handed the phone back to Chief Gray, Slade began barking out assignments. "Stella, Ander, I want you to stay here and search the house. It doesn't look like our unsub took anything obvious, but we need to see if any unobvious items are missing. Chloe, Hagen, you take Jeremy Deem's office. See if anything is out of place there. Jeremy's executive assistant, Karen Neuglass, will meet you there."

*Neuglass...glass...looking glass...Alice in Wonderland...White Rabbit...I'm late, I'm late, for a very important date.*

Was that why the Deems opened the door? They were expecting visitors?

Slade cast his gaze from one team member to another. "This is a strange one, which means the killer's unpredictable. We have to find him."

Stella thought of the dead, and how little their investigation would help them now.

*"How long is forever?" Alice asked.*

*"Sometimes, just one second."*

The White Rabbit was right. Forever for the Deem family hadn't been nearly long enough.

## 3

The security guard swiveled his chair as Hagen and Chloe crossed the reception hall of the downtown Nashville high-rise. Deem's building reminded Hagen of his father's law offices, which had been on the third floor of a place like this.

Gleaming marble shone beneath Hagen's shoes. For once, the Italian leather Oxfords he favored didn't look out of place in a criminal investigation. Floor-to-ceiling windows allowed bright natural light to fill the lobby. The place almost didn't need the fluorescents overhead.

The guard lifted a hand. "Can I help you, sir? Ma'am?"

Hagen pulled out his ID. "We're with the FBI. You were expecting us, I think."

The security guard nodded gravely. "Oh, yeah. About Mr. Deem. Man, it's a terrible thing. Murdered in his own home. And with Mrs. Deem too. People today. What happened over there exactly?"

Chloe leaned against the counter. "Nothing good. Anything you can tell us about Mr. Deem?"

He shook his head. "Uh-uh. I've been here five years.

Most he's ever said to me is 'good morning' in the morning and 'good evening' in the evening. And that's only if I say it first."

Hagen stopped next to the elevators. He pressed the up button, eager to reach Jeremy Deem's office on the ninth floor. "You wouldn't say he's a friendly type, then?"

He shrugged. "We get all types in here. Some like to stop and chat while others can't wait to get into or out of the office." He nodded toward Hagen's own obvious eagerness to head upstairs. "I don't take it personally."

Hagen jammed the elevator button, triggering an immediate *ding*. "Wise man." The doors slid apart. He stepped inside and held them open. "Coming?"

Chloe didn't move. She rested another arm on the counter. "You ever hear Mr. Deem argue with anyone? Or come in or out of the office with someone you didn't recognize?"

The security guard ran a hand under his chin, scratching at a thin beard that barely covered a heavy jowl. "No, don't think so. He'd stride right in here, eight thirty on the dot every morning. And he'd work late most days. Sometimes he wouldn't leave 'til nine, ten at night. Never understood what he did all day, but whatever it was, he did it a lot. You should talk to Karen, though. Nice lady. She's waiting for you upstairs."

Chloe thanked him and joined Hagen in the elevator. The second the doors slid shut, the car dinged and began its journey two-thirds of the way up the building. Hagen rested his back against the mirrored wall, studying their reflections, which stretched out into infinity in two directions.

"Didn't get anything out of him, huh?"

Chloe shrugged a shoulder. "Worth a try. He might have heard something if Deem liked to talk on the phone on his way in and out of the building. People like Deem talk in front of the servants." She fixed her eyes on him. "Surprised you were so eager to get away. Even a brief chat with a guard might've been useful."

Hagen didn't reply. A short burst of irritation twinged his guts. Chloe was right. He hadn't been interested in talking to a security guard. Hagen had wanted to get up to Jeremy Deem's office and find something, some clue, that would shut this case down fast. He was irked with himself.

But if they could clean this mess up now, he could put the search for the killer of Stella's father back on track. He'd talk to Stella. He'd explain helping her meant finding his own father's killer. He'd reassure her and show her she could trust him.

He could win her trust. He was sure he could.

They were *so* close.

They'd confront her father's ex-partner, the man she'd known as Uncle Joel for much of her childhood. Joel would tell them what they needed to know.

*I'll make him.*

There was no doubt in Hagen's mind that "Uncle" Joel Ramirez knew a great deal about the Memphis underworld. Joel would tell Hagen who'd ordered the death of Seth Yates.

After that, his and Stella's interests would diverge.

Stella would want justice. She'd want to see the killers arrested and charged.

Hagen had other ideas.

He knew what the courts could do. And what they couldn't.

His father's entire career demonstrated that justice was a game, one in which the player with the most funds won. The killers would get bail and throw sacks of money at a law firm in a downtown high-rise exactly like this one. The bad guys —probably crooked cops—would get off because of a lawyer arguing they had families and were public servants.

Seth Yates once had a family. Seth Yates was once a public servant.

*Vengeance.*

That was what Hagen had in mind. It was the only way. And right now, the only thing standing between him and the satisfaction of revenge was a dead financier and his family.

*We need to crack this case. Find the killer. Move on.*

First, they needed real clues. A note with a threat. Indications Deem had a jealous lover. Evidence of black-market loans the wealthy financier failed to repay despite multiple, well-documented warnings. Something. Anything.

The elevator *dinged* again, and the door slid open on the ninth floor. Hagen waited for Chloe to step out first.

A glass door directly opposite told them in bold, capital letters that they'd reached *Deem Finance*.

No tagline declared what the company did or boasted how well it did it. The logo, made up of the company's initials, gave no indication of how the company operated. It was assumed anyone who came up here knew exactly what happened behind those doors.

Chloe pushed the main door open. "Do you know what they do in places like this? I never understood what finance firms do."

Hagen half smiled. His father once spent a great deal of time in offices like these, making sure the money he earned defending clients was well-protected.

Some of it was held in a trust, keeping his mother housed and fed at a level higher than her salary as a kindergarten teacher allowed. What was left was divvied between him and his sisters, allowing one to buy a ranch and the other to go to medical school. Hagen had bought a townhouse in the city. There were plenty of reasons to be grateful to firms like Deem Finance.

"People here make rich people richer without them

having to work harder. And in return, they become rich people themselves."

Chloe waited for Hagen to pass into the office before stepping away from the door and letting it swing closed behind her. "Sounds like I chose the wrong career."

"You did. Too late now."

He stopped at the entrance to the office. It was filled with cubicles, their beige walls decorated with loose sheets of paper, printed graphs, and the occasional crayon drawings posted by proud-but-probably-absent parents.

Each desk held four monitors stacked like Legos. The screens were black now, waiting for the return of the markets on Monday morning.

A woman appeared from down the hallway and strode to the empty receptionist counter. "Hello?" She must have been in her early sixties with a wide dome of curly, orange hair above her ears. A floral summer dress that might have been in fashion a couple of decades ago hung unevenly over her square frame. The woman's nose barely reached the top of the counter, and, with the lights in the office off, she was hardly visible in the shadows.

Hagen approached the counter. "Karen Neuglass?"

She lifted her chin. "You're with the FBI?"

Chloe pulled out her ID. Karen squinted as she studied Chloe's picture and the badge next to it. She scowled harder at Hagen. "You don't have one of those?"

When Hagen pulled out his own ID, Karen nodded her approval, though her scowl didn't soften. "Been waiting half an hour for you. Mr. Deem would never have stood for that, I can tell you. Clients could see him at any hour, but if they turned up late, I'd have to book them another appointment. That's how he was. Punctual to the m-minute." Her expression dissolved into a sea of grief. She pulled a tissue out of her dress pocket and dabbed at her eyes. "I can't believe anyone would want to hurt him. It's so awful."

Chloe slipped her ID card back into the pocket of her black jeans. "How long did you work for him?"

Karen sniffed and lifted her chin. "It will be twenty-seven years this July."

Hagen lifted an eyebrow. Nashville was his sixth office in the last four years. If things worked out the way he planned, there might not be a seventh.

"He must have been a good boss if you've stayed so long."

Karen dabbed at her eye again, then blew her nose with a slimy *honk*. "He...he could be impatient, sometimes. And he had every right to be. He expected the best, and he made sure he got it. He does...did very important work in this office. And for such important people. All the best people in Kentwood trusted him with their wealth, you know. He took that responsibility very, very seriously."

Hagen nodded toward the cubicles. "I assume he didn't work at any of these stations."

Karen waved a hand, her tissue still embedded in her fist. "Oh, no. Mr. Deem didn't work here. I'll take you to his office."

She led them down a passage to a large ornate door that would have been at home in an English manse's library. Karen fished in her pocket for a key and turned the lock that opened with a loud, echoing *click*.

Hagen walked into an office that could have easily housed the twenty or thirty cubicles at the other end of the corridor. Instead of vinyl tiles, the floor was made of dark herringbone-patterned parquet, similar to what was in the man's home. A large Persian rug partially covered the wood.

Leatherbound books filled the shelves, and Hagen suspected the volumes had been bought by the yard and never opened. One wall held an eighty-five-inch television screen. The desk was a long, irregular slice of polished redwood that held a single monitor, a keyboard, and nothing else.

Chloe nodded at the desk. "You sure he worked here? Nice desk, but there's nothing on it. I wish my workspace was that clear."

Karen tucked her tissue into her pocket and offered Chloe a chilly smile. "The higher up you go in an organization, the emptier the desk. Mr. Deem spent most of his time meeting clients and assessing companies for investments. He only handled the most important people. The rest he delegated. That's why he had such a loyal and large workforce."

Loyalty was one thing, but Karen's respect for her late boss bordered on sycophancy. Hagen supposed her devotion was why Deem had kept her around for twenty-seven years.

"May we see his calendar?"

Karen's eyes widened. "You want to see his schedule?" She didn't move. Her reaction told Hagen he could've asked to rummage around Jeremy Deem's underwear drawer and received no greater shock.

He offered her his most charming smile. "I do. Mr. Deem died far too young. We need to know where your boss went, what he did, and who he met. It's the only way we can catch who hurt him and his family. Can you help us?"

Karen folded her arms. "Of course. I'm his executive assistant." She strode around the desk and jabbed a button on the keyboard. An electronic calendar populated with squares and lines of color-coded meetings. "This is his schedule. Everything is digital now."

Hagen followed Chloe around the desk for a better view. The current month's schedule was filled with line after line of appointments and meetings, some divided by gaps as short as five minutes. The screen was a patchwork of different colors, with some meetings marked in green and others in yellow, blue, and purple.

He let out a low whistle. "He was a busy man."

"He was indeed." Hagen didn't miss the note of pride in Karen's voice.

Chloe highlighted the last appointment Jeremy Deem attended. The meeting, like other meetings scattered throughout the calendar, was highlighted in green. "What was this?"

Karen squinted at the screen. Hagen wondered if she needed glasses. "That was a meeting with Mr. Ladlow. He's a new client. We haven't had him long, but Mr. Deem was already building his portfolio. All those meetings in green are client meetings."

"And the yellow ones?"

"Those are personal appointments. Anniversary dinners, ball games, the philharmonic, of course. Mr. Deem was a great supporter of the arts. He rarely missed a concert." She lowered her voice. "And if he did, he was always in a bad mood for the rest of the week. I suppose music tamed the beast." Karen's chuckle was girlishly soft.

Hagen turned the wattage up on his charm meter. "My dad was the same. Loved the opera. What are the blue and purple appointments?"

"Blue is *personal* but *necessary*. We use it for dentist appointments, meetings with Mr. Deem's own tax advisor, and so on. And the purple meetings are for potential clients, people who are likely to come aboard and need a little nudge from Mr. Deem."

Hagen stood up straight. He crossed his arms over his chest and assumed what he hoped was an executive posture. Out of the corner of his eye, he saw Karen subconsciously straighten her spine, as if preparing to take his dictation.

"Thanks so much for sharing this, Karen. Don't change anything. We'll need access to the system and to his contacts."

Karen gave a deep nod. With that instruction and her agreement, she seemed to become Hagen's own executive assistant, someone at his call and ready to do his bidding. "Yes, sir. I have your office's details. I'll send the password right away and ensure the calendar remains exactly as it is now."

"Thank you, Karen." Hagen tried to sound like an executive. The attitude didn't suit him. He felt stiff. But the strategy was working.

They left Karen in the dark office and made their long descent back to the ground floor.

Chloe watched Hagen for a moment, then laughed. "You going to take the broom out of your ass anytime soon? *Sir?*"

Hagen forced himself to relax, leaning against the mirror wall of the elevator—a move he was sure Deem would have never made. "Better?"

She checked her teeth in the mirror. "There were a lot of contacts on that schedule. Looks like Jeremy Deem met a lot of people."

Hagen shook his shoulders, chasing away the last of the executive posture. "We need to cut the list down. And we need to do it quick."

## 4

Stella let Penny Deem's pearls run through her fingers and clatter onto the dressing table. Each white ball was so smooth and so perfect. They slid over the latex of her gloves like silk. There was a way to tell whether the necklace was cultured or natural. Stella was sure if they sent the jewels to a specialist, the determination would be they were among the rarest gems in the sea.

Knots separated each individual pearl, which Stella knew meant they were real. Unlike in the movies, if someone yanked a strand of true pearls from someone's neck, the gems wouldn't scatter because each piece was tied into place. Only cheap imitations were loose. This jewelry was not imitation.

The same was true of the emerald earrings hanging inside the lid of the ornate jewelry box, the diamond necklace filling one of the box's drawers, and the ruby brooch nestled in the center of the necklace.

*Mom would love this stuff.*

Stella's mom always wore an emerald brooch, but hers was costume and inexpensive. The only genuine piece of jewelry Barbara Knox Rotenburg owned was a thin gold bracelet Stella's dad had given her for their fifth anniversary. She wore it at every memorable occasion, at the weddings of other officers at the station, at birthday meals, at anniversary dinners. The last time Stella had seen the bracelet, though, was at her brother's funeral. The gold chain had shone against her mother's black sleeve as she'd gripped Stella's hand.

She closed the box and left her gloved hand on top of the golden filigree lid.

*These shouldn't be here.*

The intruder broke into the house and killed the inhabitants but left treasures like jewels and watches lying around?

There was another box like this one in Margaret Taylor's bedroom. Penny's mother's jewelry appeared older and more ornate but was just as accessible for a thief to fence. The killer didn't even need to search or fill a bag. They'd only need to stuff the necklaces, earrings, and chains into their pockets and make their getaway.

The killer could've made twenty-five, thirty thousand dollars easy in a matter of minutes. Six figures if they took the men's watches from the walk-in closet...and yet they'd left this stuff untouched.

Stella reached for her gold ear stud, but her fingers connected with the damn protective hood again. She dropped her arm.

*Money wasn't the motive here. The killer wasn't after cash.*

And if money wasn't the motive, the case was even more unusual than the arrangement of the bodies and the bizarre rabbit mask suggested.

*Information, perhaps?*

Maybe the intruder was after some secret contract or investment plan that would be worth millions to people who understood that sort of thing. Maybe Hagen and Chloe found something at the office but hadn't had time to report it yet.

*Passion, then?*

Jeremy Deem wasn't young and handsome. But rich and successful was a combination powerful enough to attract the attention of certain beautiful young women. Maybe a peek at Jeremy Deem's schedule would reveal secret meetings with the pretty young wife of a client prone to jealousy and violence.

But Penny and Jeremy seemed solid. The two of them still shared a bedroom. Deem had opened his home to his mother-in-law. There was no reason here to suspect anything but a happy marriage.

*Revenge, then?*

Maybe Jeremy Deem or his wife or his mother-in-law had done something so terrible they'd been a target for vengeance.

Stella had seen revenge as a motive often enough. Dealers and gangbangers laid out as payment for some small slight or moment of disrespect. The desire could make people do all sorts of stupid things. Forget their friends. Ignore justice. Maybe even murder a family around a piano.

*Everything is still possible, every motive in play.*

Stella slid the jewelry box to the back of the dressing table and left the bedroom.

Ander should have moved on to the library by now. Stella descended the winding staircase to join him.

Branching off the hallway, the library was designed to appear older than the house. Two red armchairs nestled in the corner under a tall floor lamp. The deep shelves around the oak-paneled walls were filled with first editions. A formal wooden desk appeared to be a smaller replica of the Oval Office's Resolute Desk, as though Jeremy Deem's library was the command center of his own private world.

Paneled glass doors at the end of the room opened onto a stone patio.

Ander rested a hand on the top of a tall, high-end speaker next to one of the armchairs. He tilted it to get a better look. Stella cleared her throat to announce her presence.

He lowered the expensive speaker. "Find anything?"

"Sure. Boxes of jewels and a drawer full of watches that cost more than most people's homes. Just lying there. He's a strange one, our killer."

"As if the mask didn't tell us that. This speaker would be worth a pretty penny, and he left it too."

"Stranger and stranger." Stella approached the desk. "You checked this?"

Ander shook his head. "Not yet. Feel free."

Stella scooted the leather office chair out from behind the desk. Her Tyvek suit crackled as she wheeled it out of the way.

Ander turned his attention to the bookshelves. "Should make our work easier."

Stella pulled out the first drawer of the desk to find nothing but a thin pile of manila paper and envelopes. She leafed through the stationery. "What should?"

Ander turned down some books to see if anything was hidden behind them. Stella was reminded of Scooby's secret passages. "That the killer didn't take anything. Families killed because they interrupted a burglary is practically a cliché. Prisons are full of those kinds of murderers. But a killer who kills the homeowner and leaves all the valuables behind? That's unusual. This wasn't a robbery gone wrong. We're looking for someone with a grudge."

Stella pulled out another drawer. A stapler, a half-empty packet of batteries, and a lint roller. Thin blue lines squiggled across the roller's sticky surface. She closed the drawer.

"True. But I can't find a grudge in any of these drawers. I don't think he did any work here."

She ran her gloved hand over the surface of the desk. "Strange this desk is basically empty, isn't it? I mean, even if he didn't work at home very often and only used this place to sit and read, you'd expect to find books lying around or maybe magazines. Who reads books and puts them back right away?"

Ander perched on the arm of one of the chairs. "Nice place to chat, though. A real den. Friends come over. You invite the guys into your library, pour some bourbon, and sit and talk. Meanwhile, the wives gossip in the living room with the plush sofas over pots of herbal tea."

Stella snorted, unsure if he was serious. "Is that what you'd do? Leave the womenfolk behind to *gossip* so the men can have their men-talk?"

"Kelsey would've insisted. She always enjoyed gossiping—sorry, *woman-talking*—with her friends. Me? I'd have ditched the books and filled this place with pinball machines and a foosball table."

He didn't face Stella as he spoke, so she couldn't see his eyes. She wondered whether, beneath the mask of his forensic suit, his cheeks weren't reddening. His immediate silence indicated regret in talking about his ex, as though he'd opened up a little too much about a subject he didn't want to share.

Ander dropped a hand back onto the speaker. Warm piano music filled the room, the tone made richer thanks to the library's wooden walls.

"This is Schumann's *Kinderszenen*."

Stella raised her eyebrows. "Bless you?"

Ander grinned, the corners of his eyes crinkling. "I like this music. I took piano lessons when I was a kid."

Stella tried to imagine a young Ander sitting in front of

the black and white keys, curls bouncing about his shoulders as he played, face wincing whenever he missed. The picture made her smile. "Impressive. And here you are, identifying a piece of classical music. You have hidden depths."

He tapped a small screen on the top of the speaker. "Not really. It says so here. *Kinderszenen* by Schumann. Played by Antonella Romano."

Stella rolled her eyes.

The music was lovely, though. A gentle section, reminding Stella of quiet nights in front of a fireplace, gave way to a rolling sequence of rapid notes that took her to a meadow on a galloping horse on a summer afternoon.

Ander shifted his attention to the speaker near another armchair. "How'd the trip go?"

His voice brought her back to the room. "Hm? What trip?"

Ander lifted the cushion from the armchair. A silverfish scuttled into the corner. He dropped the cushion back into place. "The one to Atlanta. Didn't you go with Hagen the other week?"

Stella pulled out the desk's bottom drawer to avoid the direct question. Its collection of paper clips and ballpoint pens would do little to advance the investigation.

So Ander knew she and Hagen had gone to Atlanta. Her throat tightened in frustration.

*Was there anyone in Nashville who didn't know her business?*

And they were supposed to be keeping the investigation quiet, dammit.

She answered with her head still buried behind the desk. "Wasn't great. I wanted to dig up some family information. Hagen offered to help. We were barely there for half a day before Slade called us back for the cheerleader killings."

"Yeah, that was a rough case, that one."

"You know, if you need help with anything, feel free to ask. I'd be happy to lend a hand too. We all would."

Stella swallowed, eased the drawer closed, and peeked up at him. "Thanks. I'm just not sure I'm ready to involve too many people."

Ander gave her a small nod, not pressing.

Stella remembered what Mac had told her when they discovered Stella was being followed. They were all in this together, Mac had said then. If there was a threat to one, there was a threat to all.

But Stella hadn't seen any sign of the tail for a while.

The beat-up Toyota she'd spotted speeding away from the Chapel Island Harris Hotel a week ago hadn't turned up since. Whoever had been following her, whether they were friends of Joel Ramirez, criminals connected to her father's death, or agents from witness protection, they seemed to have given up.

Or become much better at their job. Stella wasn't sure which.

Maybe Mac was right. Maybe she should bring in Ander and Slade and Chloe and everyone else. She could never have too many eyes watching her back, and they were, after all, talking about a law enforcement issue.

She lifted her head and swallowed hard.

"But—"

*Knock.*

## 5

A rubber-clad hand tapped on the library door. A forensic tech stood in the doorway, her features hidden by her mask and hood. "There's someone here who wants to talk to the FBI. I sent them out to wait in the garden." Her voice was muffled, making it sound as if she were speaking from behind a wall.

Stella felt a small sense of relief. Her confession would have to wait.

Ander followed behind Stella as she opened the glass doors behind the desk and stepped into the hot, sticky air. Sweat immediately prickled along the back of her hairline and under her bra.

A slim man in a white shirt and dark blue jeans made his way around the side of the house. He had a long stride and a clean-shaven face, but his skin was pale, and there was a redness around his eyes, suggesting either a hard night or a difficult morning. A gold ring gleamed on his pinkie. Stella put his age somewhere in the late thirties.

He slowed as Stella and Ander stepped carefully through the library's back door, their shoe covers sliding against the patio's stone tiles. Stella put her hand on the side of the house to catch her balance.

"You two with the FBI?"

Stella pulled off a glove. "That's right. And you are...?"

Annoyance flared across his features. Was he irritated at Stella's failure to recognize him?

"I'm Jeremy Deem the Second. Jem. My parents and my grandmother are there in the...in the house."

Stella took a deep breath, inhaling the plastic scent of her suit. Talking to a relative of the victim was never easy. But the conversation would definitely produce more results than poking through half-empty desk drawers. She indicated an iron table surrounded by four chairs standing at the end of the patio. Long-stemmed roses bent over the metalwork. Under different circumstances, it'd be an ideal dinner date table.

"Why don't you take a seat? We'll be with you right away."

Jem hesitated. For a moment, Stella thought he might insist on going inside. But then he strode to the table, sat down, and buried his head in his hands.

Stella pulled down the hood of her whites and dragged off her mask. She almost groaned with pleasure. Even in the midday heat, the air was welcome against her skin. After tasting fresh air, she and Ander were out of their Tyvek in seconds and handing their foot covers to a forensic scientist for bagging.

Now she could talk to someone face to face, see their expression, and know they could see hers.

She pulled out the heavy iron seat opposite Jem and sat down. Ander took the chair next to her. Jem's eyes were closed. His head swayed in time with the music leaking through the open doors to the library.

Stella gave him a moment before prompting. "Mr. Deem?"

He opened his eyes and blinked twice. "Sorry. The music. My father always loved this piece. Schumann was his favorite composer."

Stella gave him a comforting smile. Her father had his own favorite tunes, too, but they were all by Johnny Cash, and he could never quite remember the lyrics. He'd hum his way through.

"We're very sorry for your loss. I'm sure this is a great shock. Is there anyone you can think of who might have done something like this?"

Jem rubbed the top of his shirt as if it irritated him. One thumb disappeared into his collar, scratching. "No, of course not. And I'm sure my parents didn't know anyone either."

"No enemies? No one who had a grudge?"

Jem lowered his hand. His fingers disappeared into the gaps in the table's ironwork. The man could barely keep still. "I'm sure my dad made a few enemies during his time in finance. He's shorted plenty of companies. But it's business."

Stella gave a small nod, trying to hide her disagreement. Betting against the success of a company and driving down the value of its investors' wealth could be a reason to kill. If Jeremy Deem pushed a company into bankruptcy or somehow ruined an investor, he could have made an enemy angry enough to seek revenge. Deem dealt in hundreds of millions of dollars—big grudge money.

The investors and entrepreneurs Jeremy Deem might have burned wouldn't necessarily care about fencing jewels and electronics. Deem's death would be enough.

Ander cocked his head. His blond curls were frizzy from the humidity. "You an only child?"

"Uh-huh. Doctors told my mom she couldn't have kids. Until I came along. I was her miracle baby."

"So this house, your dad's company, his savings. You'll inherit it all, right?"

Stella didn't move. Ander had moved on to the tough questioning much faster than she'd expected and much faster than she thought they should. But she didn't want Jem to see her surprise.

*Let him believe we're both grilling him.*

Jem's fingers curled around the ironwork. His knuckles whitened. A flush rose above his itchy collar. "I...I...I suppose...are you trying to imply something, Agent?"

Ander leaned back against his iron chair, physically pulling back the pressure, giving Jem space. "I'm only establishing relationships and obvious next steps. Where were you last night?"

"Me?" The red flush trickled up to his jawline. "I'll tell you where the hell I was last night, Agent. I was at my daughter's piano recital."

Ander didn't appear concerned by Jem's cursing and threatening demeanor. "And where was that?"

"About two minutes up the road. The Kentwood Music Conservatory. There were about thirty kids there altogether, plus their parents."

Stella thought about Jem's father, mother, and grandmother forced to sit through a performance in their own music room. Why were they even home if there was a loved one's concert to attend? "Your parents didn't attend their granddaughter's performance?"

Jem shook his head. "Of course they wanted to, but it's a small auditorium. Parents, siblings, and teachers only. We were supposed to stop by afterward, but my daughter was tired. So I messaged them, and we went home."

"Too tired to stop by to see her grandparents for only a moment?"

Nostrils flaring, Jem lifted a hand. "Even for a musician so young, a performance can be taxing. You see, music demands respect. Focus. Had my daughter been filled with youthful energy following the recital, I would have been disappointed in her."

Was that why the Deems didn't check their security before answering the door? They were expecting a triumphant granddaughter and got a terrorizing rabbit instead?

"Can we see that message?"

Jem rolled his eyes but pulled up his texts. He slid the phone across the wrought iron table.

Stella checked the time stamp. Jem had sent the message just past seven p.m. The front door camera footage had been around six thirty. The Deems might not have even seen the message. They were too busy being held hostage.

She handed the phone back. "Thanks. So it was you, your wife and daughter, and a whole school of people at the recital?"

"And a few local officials…like this lady."

He stood as Chief Gray came around the corner of the house.

Without her Tyvek suit, she appeared much more authoritative and attentive. Her gray hair was pulled back into a tidy bun, and her chief's hat was gripped in one hand as she strode to the table. There was a confidence in her walk, suggesting she was used to giving orders and not used to seeing them questioned.

"Jem. I'm so, so sorry."

She greeted Jem with a hug and an air kiss that missed his cheek by a good two inches. As she rubbed his upper arm, she suddenly seemed more like a favorite aunt than the local head of law enforcement.

Jem collapsed back into his seat. His fingers stretched across the table as though the furniture alone could keep him upright. "Do you know who did it, Jean?"

Stella waited for the chief's answer. Unless she was

keeping a secret that would make their work a great deal easier, she was going to have to confess they had no idea.

Chief Gray shook her head. "We'll get them, Jem. I personally called in the FBI to help. We're going to find them. How are Claire and Ellie taking the news?"

For the first time since she'd pulled off her Tyvek suit, Stella wished she was still wearing her mask. Suppressing her irritation at the chief's smooth shift of responsibility took effort. Gray managed to reassure a member of the public, avoid admitting she knew nothing, and develop plausible deniability all in one sentence. And Gray's diplomacy was working.

Jem sighed. "It's tough. Ellie was so close to her grandparents and to Mawmaw. To lose them all on the same day. And like this. It's awful."

Chief Gray crossed her arms over her chest, almost crushing her hat. "She's a strong kid, your daughter, stronger than she looks. She did so well last night. And her choice of piece! Rachmaninoff, my gosh. At her age, she played perfectly. Wonderful. She's so talented."

Jem smiled. "I don't know where she gets it from. Certainly isn't me."

Stella side-eyed Chief Gray. This was all getting to be a bit much. Law enforcement was supposed to express authority, not chitchat with persons of interest.

Chief Gray squeezed Jem's shoulder. "Listen, this isn't a great place for you right now. Why don't I have one of the men drive you home, huh? Your family has always been such a support to the department. Let us help you now."

Jem hesitated. He glanced at Ander, daring the special agent to say that he needed to stay. Chief Gray pulled Jem away before either Ander or Stella could react.

"Oh, I'm sure they'll be fine. They know where to find

you if they have any more questions. You need to be with your family right now. Let us do our work."

She led Jem away from the table and toward the corner of the house.

Ander waited until the pair was out of sight before slouching in the hard chair. "An alibi from the chief herself."

"Handy, that," Stella agreed. "But the inheritance is the closest thing we've got to a motive so far. We need to check him out."

# 6

I didn't need consolation, but Liszt's *Consolations* always inspired me. Six pieces building and shifting. Each element bending and drifting into the next. No, I needed no comfort or consolation after my performance last night. I regretted nothing.

Instead, I needed to refill my creative well. Liszt always served to remind me what one could achieve when willing to throw away conventional structure and write one's own rules. This was what genius sounded like. Once I'd realized conventions were merely limits imposed by others, I finally understood what Liszt had always known.

Anything was possible.

The "Lento Placido" began. I could only lie back on my motel bed, ignore the squeak of the mattress, and let my hands follow the music through the air, my fingers dancing with the notes. The camera would catch each movement so I could later watch my form with a critical eye. If I couldn't play for an audience, I would conduct. But not until each motion of my hand was precise.

*Bam. Bam. Bam.*

"Will you turn that crap down?"

The cheap, faded print of a sunflower broke free of its nail and crashed onto my headboard. I only managed to stop the thing from falling on my head because my hands were already in the air. Apparently, my neighbor, a large man who liked to parade around in boxer shorts and a stained undershirt stretched to accommodate his ample stomach, did not appreciate the finer things in life.

Heathens. Barbarians. Philistines who couldn't appreciate art when they heard it.

"You wouldn't recognize genius if Mozart played your entrails like a harp!" I murmured as I tossed the shoddy artwork across the room.

Against my wishes, I turned down the volume on my phone. No point in drawing attention. I didn't want to argue with the uncouth man.

Who knew what he might do to my fingers?

I dreaded physical injury to my hands. Surgeons surely had the same problem. Like me, they needed to avoid bodily altercations to continue to use their brains to achieve their goals. Plan, then execute.

Lying back on the bed, I closed my eyes.

I didn't go to sleep. Not that! Not while the music still played. But closing my eyes helped me appreciate it more, even at a lower volume. I could almost see the notes rising and falling against the insides of my eyelids.

Last night, I'd occasionally closed my eyes while playing. I couldn't help it. The music carried me away. Deem's piano was so beautiful. A real Steinway. I hadn't played an instrument of such quality in years. So much better than those Yamahas in music stores and hotel lobbies. The Steinway's tones were so rich, so full. And the audience was so appreciative.

So captive. They'd listened with rapt attention from the first note to the last.

Well, almost to the last.

The old bitch's snores ruined everything.

Those Philistines. In the end, they'd understood.

My phone buzzed on the nightstand, jarring me back to the tiny room.

"Yes."

Tapping the speaker icon, I listened to my greatest supporter commend me for a job well done. I smiled, knowing the camera would also report this praise. The words were the applause I longed for. Craved.

"You're not done, though."

I knew that. Of course I knew.

Listening diligently and taking notes, I nodded as the plan came together. Location. Audience. Timing. My greatest supporter had thought of it all.

"Do you understand?"

"Yes. Thank you."

"You're welcome. Music demands respect. Focus. And by extension, the musician deserves respect and focus too. To offer anything else is an unforgivable insult…a crime. Crimes must be punished."

And once all the transgressors received their punishment, once everyone had paid the price they owed, I would rest.

"I'm the punisher."

"Yes. You still have work to do."

As the conversation ended and the sixth consolation reached its final notes, I felt under the mattress and pulled out my piece of piano wire. I no longer owned a piano. But keeping the length of wire from my last instrument made me feel close to music wherever I was.

I stretched the metal between my hands. The steel seemed dull in the dim light of the motel room. Who could've thought such simple material, so industrial and practical, could produce such beautiful, delicate tones?

Spots of dried blood were the only sign this length of piano wire had produced anything of value as of late.

I examined the dark patterns on the steel. Soon, there would be more.

# 7

Stella was happy to leave the finicky forensic work to others but being back in the office carried its own frustrations. The sun shone through the window, and she wanted to be out there, chasing leads, interviewing witnesses—talking to family members and grilling contacts and colleagues. Since she'd started working at the Nashville resident office, the desk jockey stuff usually fell on Dani.

Not that it'd helped her during their last case.

Her pregnancy hadn't been an excuse not to do the job. In fact, Stella suspected the baby she carried was what had given her the strength to last as long as she had with her kidnapper.

She dropped her face in her hands, scrubbing away the memories.

"Quit procrastinating."

With that jolt, Stella set to work. But, dammit, she missed them. Personally and professionally. She'd gotten used to being out in the field while Dani and Mac stayed in the office and searched the databases.

But neither would be back for a while, so the computer stuff would be distributed between the rest of the team.

*Pity.*

"Knew it. Told you, Stella." Ander tapped his computer screen so hard the monitor bounced on the desk. It actually tipped before he caught it.

"What did you tell me?"

"I told you we needed to check out Jem Junior. Boy's got a record."

"Oh, yeah?" Stella rolled her chair until she could see Ander past her own monitor. "For shooting and garroting?"

"Er…no." Ander adjusted his monitor back into place, reading his screen. "Typical rich boy stuff. He was picked up twice for possession, but charges were dropped each time. Surprise, surprise."

"Not shocking."

She'd spent enough time as a police officer to see the unfairness of the law. An expensive, capable lawyer could be very convincing to D.A.s who didn't feel like prosecuting. If a poor kid was caught with the same baggie, the D.A. was "being tough on crime." With a rich kid, the same D.A. was "considering the boy's future."

Ander rolled the scrolling wheel hard on his mouse. It rattled like something was loose. Ander had all the grace of a gorilla with his computer. Everything he did was bold, heavy, forceful.

"Yeah. He's also been investigated a few times for securities fraud and insider trading."

That got her attention a bit more. "Really?"

"But again, no charges. Lucky boy. Or very unlucky, to keep being persecuted in this way. What have you got?"

Stella sighed. "Not much. He's been in and out of court-mandated rehab a few times. Currently married. He's also got an ex-wife who takes a lot of alimony and child support.

He has two kids, one with each wife. Both kids are in private schools. And then you've got the music lessons on top of the school fees, as well, I guess."

Ander let out a low whistle. "Those are big expenses. I'm glad Murphy goes to public school and likes playing frisbee. It can't be easy being rich."

Stella grinned. "Yeah, I'd hate it. Thank God it's not a problem I'll ever have."

Ander's smile mirrored hers. "Dodged a bullet there. Anyway, he's got a motive, right? Big expenses, and his giant inheritance will help him cover them. That would also explain why he didn't take the jewels and the watches. They're his now, anyway. Maybe we don't have to look any further."

Stella wasn't so sure.

"Alimony and rumors of illegal trading don't actually amount to much. Plus, it's a big step from money pressures to killing your entire family. And to do it so strangely too. There are much easier ways to kill than garroting. And then there's the rabbit mask and—"

"He'd have to wear something. His parents would recognize him."

"And he has an alibi. Confirmed by the chief herself."

"Maybe he hired someone to do it? A strange, um, bunny assassin?"

Stella spun in her office chair, letting the world shift and bend as she puzzled it out loud. "A hired gunman who wears a rabbit mask, eats his victims' dinner, and ties all three up in front of a piano because…he needed an audience? Why not just shoot them?"

She stopped spinning. The world righted itself. A hired gun didn't quite fit.

"He's a psychotic bunny with a spotlight fetish?"

Damn, he was funny.

"Why kill the grandmother? If all Jem wanted was to inherit his dad's business or only his money, his parents would have been enough. Jem probably didn't even need to do more than knock off his dad, so his mother is extra too. And garroting? That's personal. It all feels personal. Did Jem hate his dad?"

Ander laced his fingers behind his head. "I won't find that out in financial records. But…yeah…maybe. We know he's had drug problems. If we look more closely, we might find—"

The door swung open behind Ander, cutting him off mid-flow.

Hagen held the door open for Chloe, a hopeful smile lighting his face. "Find the killer yet?"

Ander shrugged. "We were just talking about that. We met Jeremy Deem's son at the house. I think he's a strong suspect. Stella thinks he's—"

"Not." She couldn't help it. Jem didn't sound right to her. Not without more background. All the arguments for Jem were reasonable and logical. Family often killed family—sad, but true. But, while this crime felt personal, it didn't *feel* familial. She couldn't articulate what nagged at her. Finally, she offered Ander a compromise. "He's a possibility, but we'd have to do a lot more digging."

As Hagen and Chloe took their seats, she waited for them to add to the conversation.

Chloe answered first, leaning back in her chair and propping her feet on her desk. "Deem had a very nice office, a cloying assistant, and could be a nasty boss."

"So can I, Chloe." The door swung closed behind SSA Slade as he strode into the office. "And I'll be a very nasty boss if you don't get your feet off the desk. You're not in your living room now."

Chloe dropped her feet to the floor. "Fat chance. Hardly seen my living room in weeks."

Slade perched on the edge of Hagen's desk. "What did you learn?"

Hagen shrugged. "Nothing much. His assistant gave us access to his calendar and his contacts. I've already sent you the password and access information. We can see who he knows and who he's been meeting."

"I saw what you sent. Anything stand out?"

"Not really. But I haven't had time to dig through it yet. Back-to-back client meetings, regular engagements at the philharmonic, and occasional trips to the dentist. It's a pretty full schedule."

Ander shifted his monitor, opening his view of everyone in the room. "Would he have had meetings not scheduled on his calendar?"

"Can't say for sure at this stage." Hagen tapped a few buttons on his keyboard. "Between his scheduled meetings, it looks like he barely had time for a sandwich. If the calendar is accurate, I'd be surprised if we find anything off the books."

"And dear Karen Neuglass probably wouldn't let Deem out of her sight anyway. It's a miracle she wasn't at the house last night, tracking his dining habits." Chloe picked out a cherry Starburst from the candy dish on her desk. She'd started smoking again on the last case as they'd searched for Dani and Mac's kidnapper. Starburst chews were Chloe's go-to replacement. Stella was pleased to see the habit hadn't stuck. Chloe's wife, Bridget, must have talked to her.

That someone could lay down the law with Chloe was something of a miracle. She kept her vulnerable side hidden at work, but Stella knew it was there.

Chloe rolled the candy wrapper between her fingers. "Are we sure Jeremy Deem was the target? There are three victims. Maybe the killer was going for one of the others, and the other two got in the way."

Slade crossed his arms over his chest, pondering. "It's a thought. And to be thorough, we need to dig into them. But Jeremy Deem received the most, um, *personal* attention. The victim the killer garroted is, statistically, the one they were most interested in."

"Sir?" Hagen scratched his forehead where frown lines had appeared.

"Yes?"

"I've got a question. Why can't the locals check these people out? Kentwood's one of the wealthiest jurisdictions in Tennessee. Why'd we get called in?"

Everyone turned to Slade.

The SSA didn't answer immediately, and Stella wondered about his hesitation. "All I can tell you is Chief Gray requested our assistance, claiming her department is stretched and doesn't have the resources to investigate something like this. We go where we're needed."

No one spoke.

Stella translated the bullshit explanation. Chief Gray, who led a department better equipped than most FBI field offices, had requested the FBI's assistance…so she'd have a scapegoat if things went wrong.

The chief had been a master of political maneuvering as she'd pulled Jem Deem from their interview a few hours ago. Gray knew exactly how to speak to her wealthiest citizens.

Next to Stella, Chloe snorted. Stella knew what she was thinking.

The rich residents of Kentwood wanted to be sure a crime in their neighborhood was getting top attention.

And Chief Jean Gray refused to be put in a position where she'd have to take the fall.

Slade removed his reading glasses from his pocket and

polished them with a small cloth. Stella saw his irritation at the situation in his tight, precise swipes.

"Eyes are on us. We can't screw this up. Not that I'd expect any of you to screw up. But do me a favor and make sure we don't screw up." He breathed on one of the lenses and polished again. "Suspects. From what I understand, all we've got is a possible in the son. But nothing solid on him yet."

Hagen lifted a finger. "Have we checked his alibi?"

"His alibi's Chief of Kentwood Police." Stella twisted in her chair but forced herself to stop. She shouldn't fidget right now. "Jem Deem was at his daughter's recital last night. With Chief Gray."

"Well, that's about as good an alibi as you're gonna get. You still think it's him, Ander?"

"Dunno." Ander shrugged at the SSA. "He could have hired someone. Man like him could afford to pay a professional killer."

Stella agreed to a point, but something still felt off. "Professionals are calm, clean, efficient. This murder is messy. And strange. I don't know many professionals who'd wear a rabbit mask. They wouldn't stop to take a dinner break either. They'd do the job and leave. Three double-taps and gone."

"Maybe he's not a very good professional." Chloe grinned. "A cheapo weirdo hired on the dark web?"

Stella ignored Chloe's sarcasm but seized on her salient point. "Even a bad professional would need intelligence, right? We should check cameras around the house and Deem's office."

"We're already checking the camera footage." Hagen sounded mildly insulted that she might suggest they *hadn't* already done so.

"I mean, over the past couple weeks, a pro would have

staked him out. Followed him around before picking his moment."

Stella swallowed against a sudden lump in her throat. Over the past few weeks, she'd worried about being followed, tailed, staked out. Maybe the person tracking her hadn't stopped. Maybe they were getting better at it. Picking their moment. Watching her from a distance. Deciding when to make their move.

A chill passed down her spine. She couldn't keep this situation a secret much longer.

Slade lifted his hand, cutting off further speculation. "We're getting ahead of ourselves. Let's put the hitman theory on the back burner for now. At least until we get, you know, *evidence*. One step at a time." He pocketed his now sparkling reading glasses. "Hagen, Chloe, first thing in the morning, I want you two to talk to Candice Diaz, the Deems' housekeeper. She found the bodies. Few people will have more insight into their lives than her. I'll ask Martin and Caleb to see what they can find about Margaret and Penny Deem."

Chloe replied with a quick thumbs-up.

"Stella, Ander, I want you two to stay on Jeremy Senior. Let's see if he made any enemies or has anything else to hide."

Ander scrunched up a ball of paper and tossed it over the desk at Hagen. "Send me the password for the calendar?"

The ball bounced off Hagen's chest and landed on the floor next to Slade's feet. The SSA picked up the missile and squeezed it between his fingers. "No need for that." He paused. "Mac's already on it."

A jolt of surprise and joy surged through Stella. "Mac? She's working?"

"I stopped off at the hospital on the way back to see how she's doing. I told her about the case, and she dug in, right there in her hospital room. She also thinks she might have something. She'll be here soon."

The door opened, and Mac's bruised and bandaged face greeted them with a broad smile.

"Or I'll be here right now."

## 8

Tracking FBI Special Agent Stella Knox was a challenge and a pleasure. Every one of Sis's skills was put to the test as she'd followed Agent Knox over the past two days. She'd stood at a distance while the FBI and local sheriff's deputies tore apart the wooded areas around Pelham County, hunting for a killer determined to lay waste to government employees.

*More power to him.*

But none of those agents or cops spared her a sideways glance. Of course, Sis had stayed back, out of sight and out of mind.

That had been Junior's mistake—being seen. Poor boy. He'd always had more heart than brains.

And no guts at all.

Sis had guts. She had *gumption*, as her boss, The Officer, said. Sis was capable of anything. And she was quite proud of this trait.

*Hell, I killed my own brother right outside another crime scene.*

Sis lay back on Special Agent Stella Knox's bed and folded her arms behind her head. She smiled at the memory.

Killing Junior had been glorious. She'd followed him out to that little suburban house and found him skulking in the bushes, watching the action, as usual.

The backyard garden had been smeared with some teenager's blood. Stella Knox, the agent herself, had been busy capturing a nutjob cheerleader killer.

Once upon a time, Sis had been a cheerleader as well, so she understood that having a competitive edge was necessary. While the federal officers were busy, Sis seized the moment.

Junior had been too scared to move, the idiot. He'd made the whole thing easier.

The look on his face when she'd lifted the gun and put him right in the middle of the sights…

He didn't think she was going to do it. She could tell he thought she was joking like they'd joked when they were kids. She'd often aimed their father's rifle at him, sworn it was loaded, and then watched his face pale as she pulled the trigger.

*Pale? He was as white as a fish's belly.*

But she hadn't been joking that time.

*Tap-tap.*

His chest exploded right after she'd taken the first shot. No matter how many times she relived it, she never tired of the memory.

Telling The Officer what she'd done was priceless.

Now there was no more competition, and The Officer knew he could trust her. This job was hers now, all the way. As it always should have been.

She stretched her arms, dragged the pillow around, and buried her face in it.

Lavender shampoo with a touch of vanilla.

*How sweet. Turns out Special Agent Stella Knox is a girly girl when she's all alone.*

Sis could take her time. The news reported mysterious deaths in the Kentwood area. Rich people were more demanding. Stella would be gone for hours.

She put the pillow back in place and rolled off the bed. Sis tugged the wrinkles out of the comforter.

Stella's apartment was so neat and cozy. Sis had only been there once before, sneaking in for the briefest of recons. A little red sofa sat at an angle near the window. The clock next to the bed had big, bright numbers. The kitchen was neat as a pin, with its wiped-down counter and little fish tank. Such a pleasant place to live.

It was good to be here again. Sis felt more in tune with the federal agent here. Much more so than following her around, watching her shop or jog in the park or visit one of her teammates in the hospital. There wasn't much to learn from the day-to-day activities.

And there was so much Sis needed to learn.

*What did Stella Knox know about Joel Ramirez, and who else had she told?*

As Sis had sat in the café downstairs that morning, watching Stella order her brunch, she'd heard the agent get one call, then another. During the first conversation, Stella's expression was curious and concerned. The next call had sent her to her feet and off to Kentwood.

Stella hadn't even stayed to finish her food.

Sis had tailed her to the Richie Rich neighborhood before deciding the agent's empty apartment was too good an opportunity to pass up.

If Stella was working a case, she wouldn't have time to deal with her own business. And Kentwood was full of security cameras and guards at the best of times. Not a place someone like Sis should be seen.

She hoped whoever Stella was chasing got themselves a

good haul before they left. They'd done her a real solid. "Thank you, stranger. And now, to work."

Under the bed, Sis found only dust bunnies and a couple of dimes. She pocketed them. The drawer in the bedside table held a barely used tube of moisturizer and a small jewelry box containing no jewels. Sis was surprised to find a worn police badge.

She pulled it out and sat on the edge of Stella's bed, wrinkling the comforter again.

The number 1372 still shone at the top of the shield despite the wear. Sis weighed it in her hand.

"Aww, was this your daddy's?"

She put the badge on her breast and spoke in a deep voice. "I'm Sergeant Knox, and you're under arrest." She gasped dramatically. "Oh, no, please don't shoot me. Aaagh!" She fell back onto the bed. She aimed her finger at the middle of the shield and squeezed an imaginary trigger twice.

"Cops, man. Think they're the bee's knees until they meet someone with a bigger sting."

Sis laughed and dropped the badge back into the box. She closed the lid and slid the drawer closed.

At the desk by the wall, Sis powered up Stella's laptop. The home screen asked for a four-digit passcode.

Stella's birthday was June first, but 0601 didn't work.

Sis looked back to the drawer she'd just closed.

Dad's badge number. 1372.

*Access denied.*

She slammed the lid shut and dropped the machine back into place, muttering as she did so.

"Damn computers. Always hated geek stuff. More trouble than it's worth."

A television stood on a dresser at the end of the bed. Sis turned it on. The screen opened to Netflix. She scrolled through the shows Stella had been watching. *The Queen's Gambit. Maid. Dream Home Makeover.*

Sis sat on the mattress and scrolled down the page. "No cop shows, Stella? Too much like being at work? Still, I wouldn't have put you down for a home makeover kinda girl." She glanced around the fairly plain apartment. "You do surprise me."

She turned off the television and put the controller back exactly where she'd found it, adjusting the angle so Stella wouldn't notice anything had been moved.

In the kitchen, the fridge held a jar of mayonnaise and enough Korean takeout to last a week.

The freezer contained only a frozen pizza with olives. "No pepperoni? No pineapple? Girl, you need to loosen up. You don't even let yourself go when you're at home. And for chrissakes, get yourself some ice cream."

She closed the freezer door and leaned on the counter. A lone fish darted around the stone bridge in the tank on the edge of the countertop. Sis rested her chin on the back of her hand and watched it swim.

"You're a cute little fellow, aren't you?" She tapped on the glass. "Let's make a deal, you and me, fish. You don't tell anyone I've been here, and I won't tell anyone you had a little snack."

She opened the fish food and sprinkled a generous pinch over the water's surface. The fish darted up and swallowed one mouthful after another.

"I think we got ourselves a deal."

She put the fish food back on the counter, turning the tube so the label faced outward.

"All right, let's finish up."

From her leather bag, Sis removed a device that looked like the cover of an electrical socket. She prized the real socket off the wall and replaced it with her own. The tiny microphone was hidden inside the case. She replaced the clock on the bedside table with an identical copy, except for the little lens in the center of the face, where the hands met.

"You should really get some original pieces, Stella. But I'm so glad you buy mass-produced crap. I'd hate to spend a lot of money on some expensive alarm clock."

When she was done, Sis sat on the edge of the bed facing the window.

She pulled her phone out of her bag and dialed. The number rang once, twice, before the answer came.

"What?" As usual, The Officer's voice was curt and angry. Sis ignored the tone. The Officer always sounded as though his dinner was interrupted.

"There's nothing here. I've planted the bugs. If she talks, we'll know."

The Officer was silent. Sis swallowed. She hoped he wasn't disappointed. Surely he couldn't be.

"All right. You've done better than your idiot brother, anyway."

Sis grinned. "You know those bugs won't be of any use if Stella doesn't talk when she's at home."

"Yeah." The Officer's voice was a growl. "So you'd better check what the others know, especially that Hagen Yates and the other one, the blond. And any of the others too."

Sis sighed. She lay back against Stella's bed and stretched an arm across the covers. "Yeah, okay. You know, Boss, it would be a lot easier if I just killed her now."

Silence was like a scream before he answered. "All in good time, kid. All in good time."

## 9

Stella jumped up from her chair so fast the wheels shrieked as they scratched across the floor. She reached the front of the room and hugged Mac, not caring if the whole team watched. But it was immediately clear the team didn't care because everyone rushed forward and joined in a large group hug. Only Slade held back, but Stella caught him smiling.

"All right, all right!" Mac laughed as she pushed everyone away.

A large bandage covered one side of the cyber sleuth's forehead. Scratches decorated one cheek and the bridge of her nose. The right side of her jawbone was a delicate shade of yellow and purple. She grinned at Stella as everyone else pulled away. "Wanna go check out our victim's calendar?"

"I'd love nothing more."

"Let's go."

At first, it seemed like the whole team would crowd into Mac's office.

Slade put a stop to that. "Stella and Ander, go with Mac.

The rest of you have your assignments. There'll be plenty of time to catch up with Mac after we nab this creeper."

From the corner of her eye, Stella saw Hagen straighten, looking like he might argue, before turning away. What was he so frustrated about?

Stella and Mac walked down the corridor to the tech agent's office, arm in arm. It was great to feel Mac, solid and real, beside her. She'd missed her friend and colleague. Stella also couldn't help but notice the small sigh of relief Mac released when she sat at her desk chair.

She was still in pain.

Despite her wounds, her fingers flicked across the keyboard as though today were just another day. It was as if surviving a car crash and being kidnapped and waterboarded by a serial killer was on par with a rough night at a dive bar.

Once they were alone, Stella's joy at seeing Mac gave way to worry. Mac couldn't have recovered this quickly, not from all she'd been through. Stella wasn't entirely sure *she'd* recovered herself.

"What are you doing here?"

Mac shrugged, a wince following the movement. "Working. Like you guys."

"Like us? We didn't just go through hell." Stella planted her hands on her hips. "As happy as I am to see you, you should be resting. You should be in bed, watching television and reading trashy magazines, not...sitting here at your computer."

"She's not wrong."

Stella whirled to find Ander leaning against the doorjamb. "Don't sneak up on me like that!"

He grinned, then his expression turned serious when his focus returned to Mac. "You should be taking time off. You've earned it. I mean, it's good to see you up and about, but maybe you should stay down and out for a while?"

Mac waved away their concern and turned her attention to the pair of monitors dominating her desk. "*Pshaw.* Hair of the dog. Back in the saddle. Blah, blah, blah. What can I say? I missed you guys."

"You haven't had time to miss us." Stella lowered her voice, a quiet rebuke for her friend to take better care of herself. This couldn't be healthy. Mac wasn't going to recover like this. She needed to talk with a counselor, process what she'd been through, and let her wounds heal. She wouldn't get better in an FBI office investigating more murders.

Mac squirmed in her seat, her attention on her monitors. "I'd rather work. Keeps my mind off stuff, you know?"

She jiggled her mouse as though she needed the constant movement to keep her screen lit and alive. "Your guy had a pretty busy life. Jeremy Deem seems to have spent most of his time bouncing from one meeting to another."

Stella let the change of subject slide. Maybe Mac was right. Sometimes it was better not to think.

"Let me see." Ander squeezed past Stella and squatted on Mac's other side, his elbow on the arm of her chair.

A pinkish rush of color rose to Mac's cheeks. It clashed with her bruises.

Stella tried not to smile. Maybe Ander was the reason Mac had come back so quickly. Even the cutest of doctors had nothing on him.

He studied the screen. "It's a colorful calendar, that's for sure."

On the monitor, strips and blocks of green, yellow, blue, and purple filled the calendar. There was barely a space between them.

Stella squatted, mirroring Ander, to get a better look. "Looks like Tetris. Though I'm pretty sure you could have handled this in your hospital bed."

The redness faded from Mac's cheeks. She was back,

mind focused on her screen. "Ha! Slade would have never given me access to this stuff in my hospital bed."

"What've we got?"

"Jeremy Deem was a busy bee." Mac's finger drifted to the yellow strips dominating the schedule after work. Each night held at least one strip. Some contained as many as three, with one event beginning before the previous had ended. "He went to a lot of dinners, attended plenty of fundraisers where he no doubt wrote giant checks for very good, tax-deductible causes, and boogied down at quite a few parties."

"Boogied?" Ander frowned at the screen. "Gotta say, when I saw him, he didn't look like the boogying type."

"Eh, who knows what financial folks do when we're not watching? He went to a lot of parties anyway. This last Saturday—*his* last Saturday—was unusually quiet. There aren't many blank spaces in his calendar, but that was one of them."

Stella thought for a moment. "Maybe he was planning to go to his granddaughter's concert, and when he found out the auditorium was too small for extras, he was left with a gap in his schedule."

"That could make sense." Mac pushed her chair back a few inches.

Her movement almost unbalanced Ander, who barely managed to catch himself before tipping over. His knees popped as he pushed to his feet. "It's certainly not like him to be sitting at home on a Saturday night. You think the killer just got lucky? Found him at home on the one night of the month he didn't go out?"

"Not likely." Stella twisted the gold stud in her ear. "The killer must have known Deem would be home. He was either close enough to know Deem's schedule or watched Deem closely enough to take the opportunity when it arose." And he'd monitored his victim without Deem noticing. "Or he stalked him."

The thought of being watched sent a shiver down the back of Stella's neck.

Mac glanced at her, worry written on her face.

"Or we could be talking about someone who knew him well." Ander bobbed his eyebrows. "Like his son."

Stella frowned. "I—"

He raised both hands in surrender, stopping Stella before she could disagree. "Okay, okay. But if it's not Jeremy Junior, then maybe we should target someone else in Deem Senior's social circle, someone who knew what he did and where he went. He must have talked to dozens of people each week. We need to determine his close friends. Mac, is there any one activity on his calendar he did regularly?"

"Like volunteering at a soup kitchen?"

Stella grinned. The man who'd lived in the Kentwood estate would have been happy to write a five-figure check to a soup kitchen...as long as he could deduct it from his taxes. But the thought of Jeremy Deem doling out ladles of minestrone to homeless people struck her as funny.

Ander ignored Mac's off-base suggestion. "I was thinking more of a gentleman's club or a round of golf."

Mac scrolled back a few weeks on the calendar. Stella blinked against the swirl of colors moving across the screen. "No golf. But the Kentwood Philharmonic turns up regularly. He sat on the board, which only happens for very generous donors. The Deems attended about once a week during the season. Sometimes more."

Stella withheld a wince. She liked most kinds of music but sitting through that many hours of classical would bore her to tears. "Sounds...fun."

Mac smirked and opened a separate file. Two columns of names filled the screen. Over half of them were shaded in green, the rest in red. "I cross-checked the names of other donors to the philharmonic with the names in his company's client list. There's a big overlap. Green means the person is on both lists."

Stella snapped her fingers, finally feeling that they might be going somewhere. "He was probably using the philharmonic to recruit clients. As a board member, he'd have access to the donor list. He'd know they had money. Shared interest in music gave him a personal connection. That's a smart way to land leads."

Mac rolled her head. "Ethically questionable, but smart. Guess that's why he's rich, and we're not. If we're looking for people who knew him well, the Kentwood Philharmonic would be a good place to start. Hey, maybe you'll find the conductor bumped him off for pitching deals during the concerts."

Ander patted Mac on the shoulder, leaving his hand near the nape of her neck. Her cheeks turned a light shade of pink again...even as she winced at the touch. "At least we'll see how he operated and what people thought of him there. If he rubbed someone the wrong way, there's a good chance we'll find out. It's good thinking, Mac."

Stella smiled at her friend. "We'll talk to the director of the philharmonic first thing tomorrow."

The room fell silent. Mac's gaze met Stella's and hung on. The look told Stella she had more to say but wanted to say it in private. The silence dragged. No one spoke.

Ander shoved his hands in his pockets.

"Right. I'll erm...I'll go and dig up some contacts. I'll leave you two to it." He winked. "You can talk about me while I'm gone."

When the door closed behind him, Stella flopped into the chair on the other side of Mac's desk. "That was very considerate."

"Considerate *and* dreamy." Mac rubbed the back of her neck where Ander's hand had been. "If the FBI would let him grow those blond curls a little longer, he'd be perfect."

"Almost."

Mac folded her arms on the desk. "Yeah, yeah. I know. You've got a different type."

Stella squashed the flash of Hagen that popped into her mind.

Mac leaned closer and lowered her voice. "Any more about that car? The one following you?"

Despite all Mac had endured, despite all she'd suffered, she wanted to talk about Stella's troubles. If it wouldn't have hurt, Stella would have given her a big hug again.

"No tail that I've seen. Maybe I'm just not as interesting as I think I am."

Mac's eyebrows rose. "Maybe you're just not as observant as you think you are."

That stung a little, even though the thought had occurred to Stella too.

If she was still being followed, whoever was doing it had upgraded from one guy in a beat-up Toyota. Spotting a more professional tail wouldn't be easy.

Mac ran a hand over her left wrist. A thick, red line marred her pale skin where she'd been bound with duct tape. The wicked line would fade eventually. But what scars would remain, Stella couldn't say.

Mac stopped rubbing but left her hand over the mark. "Stella, there were two of us in that car, and Dani's been doing this for more than a decade. Neither of us saw anything, not a damn thing, not until it was too late. We were lucky to get out of there alive. If it hadn't been for you and Hagen and…" Her voice caught.

"Oh, Mac." Stella came around the desk and wrapped an

arm around her friend's shoulder again. Her forehead touched Mac's temple.

Mac pulled away. "Ow. Ow."

Stella released her. "Sorry. I—"

"It's okay. My neck…it's still a bit sore." She straightened her spine slowly and exhaled. "Look, I'm just saying you can't do this alone. And Hagen and me? We're not enough. It took a whole team to get Dani and me to safety. It will take the entire team to keep *you* safe. At least bring Ander in. I need another pair of eyes on your back."

Mac was right. Stella knew she was. But there were so many people involved in her personal business already. First Mac, then Hagen. Now Ander too?

"Maybe. Let me think about it."

Mac gave her a small nod. She didn't look convinced. "Okay. But think hard. In the meantime, I'll see what else I can learn about Joel Ramirez."

Stella rubbed her eyes as if she could wipe away Joel's face. "Or whatever his real name is. All I know is Uncle Joel, the man and his barbeque."

Mac smiled. For a moment, the events of the last few days fell away. The old Mac was there, fun loving, scarless, and carefree.

"Maybe I'll be able to dig up his secret barbeque recipe for you. There are no limits to my research skills."

Stella headed for the door. As her fingers closed around the handle, she stopped. "How do you plan to do that research? Joel's probably in witness protection with a billion layers of confidentiality between him and us. Do I even want to know how you've found out so much already?"

Mac massaged the muscles of her sore neck. "What can I say? Even desk jockeys have their secret sources. Can't leave them all to you field people. Get some rest and stay safe."

Stella couldn't imagine what source would give Mac such

confidential information. But she was right about getting some rest. She'd tackle the Kentwood Philharmonic tomorrow morning.

And as for staying safe, Mac took the words right out of her mouth.

## 10

The frisbee sailed out of Hagen's hand. It skimmed over the emerald-green grass before angling upward, passing over the heads of two women enjoying the early evening rays, and catching the breeze.

"Go on, Bubs. Go get it."

Bubbles, Hagen's boxer and pit bull mix, raced away from beside his owner's legs. Bubs bounced across the lawn, his muscular torso giving him an uneven, thumping gait while his tongue lolled out of the side of his mouth, flapping in the air like a wet flag in a gale.

The frisbee drifted down the side of the hill.

Bubs picked up speed as he lolloped down the slope. The frisbee was just a few feet above the ground now. Bubs was almost there.

He leapt, his jaws opening. A string of thick, white saliva swung from his mouth as he flew across the grass, eyes bulging. His jaw closed with a snap.

But the frisbee bumped against Bubs's nose and dropped edge-first onto the park's thick grass.

The dog's eyes grew wide in confusion...then realization.

He rolled down the slope once, twice, three times before landing on his back. He stood up, shaking himself. Bobbling after the frisbee, he picked it up and trotted proudly back to Hagen.

Hagen dropped to his haunches and took the missile from his dog's jaws. "You are a useless mutt, aren't you?"

Bubs barked, willing to go again, but he was panting hard.

Hagen pulled his arm back, ready to throw it, but stopped. His dog gazed up at him, his broad chest billowing in and out. Hagen shook his head. "Sure you don't want a break?"

A bench stood in the shade of an elm tree behind them. Hagen walked back to it and dropped onto its slats, setting the frisbee on the seat beside him. Bubs collapsed at his feet with a satisfied huff, still panting.

The park was busy. The worst of the day's heat had burned off, bringing out joggers and outdoor yoga classes. A small family sat on the grass in front of Hagen. The mother held the back of her toddler's shirt, preventing the little one from crawling onto the dirt path nearby.

Two shirtless men tossed a football. The ball spun, its tip wobbling slightly before one of them caught it with a satisfying slap.

All around Hagen, people led normal lives. They woke up late on Sunday mornings and enjoyed pancakes or waffles before spending the rest of the morning reading a magazine or washing their cars. Today, they enjoyed the last of their weekend before heading back to their jobs tomorrow. They saved their money and counted down the days until they could retire and take their boat onto the lake or drive their RV across America.

Simple lives and simple dreams.

Those simple things so far from him.

Hagen rested his elbows on his knees and scratched his dog's head.

"I should be in Atlanta, Bubs. I should have my fingers around Joel Ramirez or whatever-his-name-is-now's throat. I should know the name of my dad's killer."

His dog didn't reply. Bubbles closed his eyes, still panting. He was used to hearing Hagen talk aloud.

"Instead, I'm stuck here dealing with the death of some rich dude who probably pissed off the wrong person. What have we got here, eh, Bubs?"

Bubs gave a low woof as if to say, "You tell me."

Hagen answered. "We've got a guy who goes to client meetings and concerts and fundraisers. His son's the biggest beneficiary of his death, but his alibi's rock solid."

Bubs farted.

"Right. And there's no sign he's in deep enough financial poop to want to bump off his whole family. So now do you know what we have to do?"

Bubs licked his balls.

"Yep. We have to drag through his very long list of contacts to find the poor sucker he annoyed." Hagen sat back and stretched an arm over the back of the bench. "Let's hope we catch him fast, huh? Then *I* can get back to work."

An agreeing bark answered him.

His phone beeped. He pulled it out, but the name on the screen disappointed him. It wasn't Stella.

Amanda, his sister, was inviting him up to the ranch next weekend. He hadn't been there for more than three months now.

He'd like to see Amanda and Brianna, his other sister. But next weekend? If he was lucky, next weekend, he'd be in Atlanta with Stella picking up the last piece of information he needed.

He brought up his contacts list. Stella's name topped the

list of recent calls. Only that morning, he'd spoken to her. Slade had called them onto the case before he could drive over and explain why he wanted to confront "Uncle Joel."

"Maybe I should do it now. What do you think, Bubs? Just do it on the phone?"

Bubbles dropped his head onto his paws and closed his eyes. Clear disagreement.

Hagen defended his position. "I don't have long, you know. We should be able to wrap this case up pretty fast. Stella might be planning to go to Atlanta next week, and I need to be there. She could scare that sonofabitch right back into hiding. And then I'll never find him. I hope we haven't scared him already."

Bubs didn't respond.

He sighed. Maybe he should go without Stella. Tell Slade he was sick and head straight down to Atlanta now. Get to Joel Ramirez before Stella. He'd come this far. Surely he deserved to take this one last step.

But even though he'd been waiting so long, moving alone felt *off*.

In the three weeks since Stella joined the Nashville office, Hagen had made more progress on his case than he'd made in three years. And it was all down to Stella and Mac. He couldn't risk cutting himself off from them.

His finger hovered over Stella's phone number. He wanted to push it. He did. All he needed to do was turn on the charm. He could do that.

But maybe he shouldn't. She had good instincts, that Stella Knox, and she was right not to trust him. They might be on the same side for now, but if push came to shove, he would always put his agenda before hers. The last thing he wanted was for the bastards who took his dad to forever extend their trial dates, or worse, get off on some random technicality.

"Son of a..."

Hagen shoved the phone back into his pocket and picked up the frisbee again. Nudging Bubs awake, he threw it as hard as he could. Bubs lifted his head and watched it fly. Slowly, he pushed himself to his feet and trotted after it.

Hagen shook his head. "You're a lazy bum. You really are."

A woman jogged past. She was slim and fit. Her long, light-brown ponytail bounced between her shoulder blades, brushing the back of her sports bra.

Bubs loped across her path as he returned with the frisbee in his mouth. She paused mid-stride and grinned at the dog. Upon seeing his owner, she smiled even wider.

Hagen smiled back and held her gaze. A flicker of electricity passed through him. It had been a while since he'd flirted with anyone. He'd been focused on Stella.

*Work. I've been focused on work.*

The jogger was traditionally pretty. She was taller than Stella and had lighter hair. Still, there was something energetic and focused about this jogger. The intensity of her gaze reminded him of Stella. The electricity gained some voltage.

"Hi." He took the frisbee from his dog's mouth and threw it again, harder this time.

Bubs trotted after it, even slower this time.

The woman stopped next to the bench, her hands on her hips. "Nice dog."

"Yeah. He's all right. Thick as a brick but nice."

She grinned. "Dogs are supposed to make us feel good about ourselves, even the thick ones. What's his name?"

Hagen examined her features. Exercise had brought a healthy color to her cheeks, but she was barely breathing hard. She was probably a former high school or college athlete of some kind.

A bright curiosity illuminated her gaze. She was sharp-minded, this woman, as well as attractive. She really was like Stella.

"Bubs."

Her eyebrows rose. "Bubs?"

"My sister named him. I've been trying to take it back ever since."

"Siblings can definitely make questionable choices. What does your sister call you?"

"Hagen. It's my name. You have siblings?"

"*Had* one. A brother. He passed away."

Hagen blinked. She said it so matter-of-factly. "I'm sorry for your loss."

*I hate that sentence.*

"Thank you. At least he didn't suffer. I hold on to that." She offered a smile, taking away the sting of awkwardness. "But he did call me plenty of things. Siblings, right?"

"What'd he call you?"

"Sam." The woman extended her hand.

Hagen squeezed but immediately realized he didn't need to be too gentle. Her grip was firm and straightforward.

Bubs ambled back, the frisbee hanging at an angle from his mouth. He dropped the disc onto the ground and flopped under the bench.

Hagen withdrew his hand and watched the dog pant heavily.

Sam rested her hands on her knees and peered under the bench. "And it's nice to meet you, too, Bubs. Don't get up. I'm not staying."

She jogged off, only slowing to turn and run backward for a few paces. "Maybe I'll see you again, Hagen."

Hagen waved, wondering if he wanted to. "Maybe you will, Sam. Maybe you will."

## 11

Stella eased back in her theater seat, rubbing her finger against the nap of the red velvet upholstery.

Rows of seats stretched on forever, and every seat was full. Men wore suits and ties. The women were decked out in ball gowns and pearl necklaces. Stella wore a long, fitted navy dress. The brooch above her left breast was her mother's, a costume copy of a Tiffany emerald surrounded by small studs of cubic zirconia.

The stage was dark. A single spotlight shone on the back of a pianist's head, highlighting the keyboard of his grand piano. His fingers floated across the keys.

The music was calm and relaxing. The slow pace of Satie's Gymnopédies took Stella to a rainy Sunday afternoon in winter. This was music for warming hands on mugs of hot cocoa and watching raindrops run down windowpanes.

Stella relaxed her shoulders and closed her eyes, allowing the music to wash over her.

Something tickled the skin of her throat. Stella lifted a hand to brush it away. Her fingers touched something thin and metallic, like a fine necklace. It tightened, slipping out from between her finger and thumb and closing around her neck.

*Wire.*

*Sharp, cutting pain seared through her throat. Her fingers scratched at steel. She dug into her own skin, trying to tear or break the garrote that threatened to sever her head from her neck. Her nails broke with the effort to get it loose.*

*Stella gasped, but no air came to her lungs.*

*The wire tightened.*

*Her tongue dropped back into her throat.*

*Wet, slippery blood ran down her neck and over her chest, soaking into her dress. Still, Stella's fingers scratched at the wire, trying to find their way under the metal, digging into the wound. Desperate, she kicked against the seat in front of her. Her elbows bashed into the arms of the listeners on either side of her.*

*No one moved.*

*The audience fixated on the pianist slogging his way through Satie's piece.*

*Stella tried to suck in air. Her throat rattled.*

*Her chest burned and her eyes bulged.*

*The pianist hit hard down on a chord in C# major.*

Ring.

*He hit it again.*

Ring.

Stella jerked up in bed, her hand on her throat. In a panic, she tried to inhale. Air rushed into her lungs.

A dream. Just a dream.

She checked the clock. Only eight p.m. She must've dozed off after dinner.

Classical music still played from her phone. The genre wasn't usually her thing, but all the philharmonic talk surrounding the case had ignited her curiosity.

Rubbing her throat, she doubted she would ever be in the mood again.

*Ring.*

A call was still coming in. She lifted the phone, stopped the music, and took the call.

"Hel…" She coughed. "Hello?"

The sound of Mac's voice was more welcome than an entire symphony. "Hey, didn't wake you, did I?"

"Wake me? No." She swiped the last bit of sleep from her eyes. "Just getting ready to go out and paint the town red."

"You're early. Things won't get going for at least a couple of hours yet. I'd join you, but…I think it'll be a while before my dancing shoes get another workout."

"Right." Stella fought the wave of pity for her friend. Mac loved to go out and socialize.

"I've got some news." Mac's voice rose, her excitement evident. "Dani had her baby! Mother and…drumroll, please…*daughter*…are both doing great."

Relief washed through Stella. Her dream, the case, the hunt for her father's killer were all swept away. It was as though someone had flung open a window and let in a beam of sunshine.

Healthy mother and healthy baby, despite everything they'd been through.

"That's great news! Have you spoken to her?"

"Not yet. She just texted. I messaged Slade. It's nice to get some good news for once."

"Yeah. Maybe we should all have babies all the time. Keep the good news flowing."

Mac laughed. "You first. I intend to enjoy myself for a while yet. Eventually. For now, all I want to do is sleep. And work, of course."

"Of course."

Sleep and work weren't enough. Mac's scars would need more than a bandage, a pill, and the distraction of an investigation to heal. A crash, a kidnapping, and torture left marks that went more than skin-deep.

"When you want to talk, I'll be here."

The other end of the call was silent, aside from a soft noise that made Stella think Mac was choking back tears. "I know. Thanks. I'm fine. Honest."

"I'm here anyway."

She felt Mac's hesitation before her friend continued in a lower voice. "I've got an appointment with the FBI's therapist next week."

Stella rolled off her bed. She squeezed the phone between her shoulder and her ear. That news was almost as good as Dani's. "Good."

"But for now, I want to work."

"The therapist will help, I'm sure."

"Yeah. I guess. Maybe you should try it too."

Stella snorted. She'd lost track of the number of hours she'd spent in a therapist's chair. First talking about her dad, then her brother.

It helped, no question. But it wasn't enough.

She rested the edge of her hand against the window to block the streetlight and peered down at the street. The café below her apartment was full, all the seats on the sidewalk taken. Cars drifted down the road. The search for a parking space kept their speed at a snail's pace.

The city had slipped into its Sunday night clothes, relaxed and happy. To Stella, that sense of ease felt so far away.

"You know what would help me? Finding my father's killer and bringing him to justice. An army of therapists couldn't have as much impact." Stella dropped her hand and stepped away from the window. She perched on a kitchen stool.

In his aquarium on the countertop, Scoot the goldfish poked his head under the bridge, drifted away, then returned to the same spot. His nighttime routine.

She sprinkled some food into the water. The particles

floated along the surface. Scoot swam up toward them, then flicked his tail and shot across the tank to nose among the stones along the bottom.

"Not hungry, huh? You're a strange little beast."

Stella closed the tube of feed. "Seeing Joel was only the start. My gut tells me he doesn't only know who helped my father's murderer. I think he knows who ordered the hit. I want him to tell me. And he will."

Mac sighed. "At least you know what you want."

"Yeah, lucky me." She knew what she wanted. Justice was always at the forefront of her mind. Bringing the guilty parties to stand trial felt right to her, but it wasn't a need for revenge. Unlike some people. "I wish I knew what Hagen wanted. Why he's so keen to help me."

"I think I know why. And if you don't know by now…"

Stella bristled. "Oh, please."

Her irritation didn't last long, though. Mac might be right. Maybe Hagen's interest went beyond a desire to help nail the killer of a friend's father, but she couldn't think about that. Not now. Not until she was done.

"It doesn't matter." She gave herself a mental shake. "Whatever I want and whatever Hagen wants will have to wait. We've got a killer bunny to find."

## 12

Donovan Freeman sat in his home theater, his favorite place. The space held twelve plush seats, each the size of a large armchair. Yet Donovan sat alone. He flipped the page of his *National Geographic* and swirled his glass of Chateau Canon 2015. He sniffed and sipped, drawing air over the grapes.

He frowned.

For two hundred and fifty bucks a bottle, the Bordeaux should have had more body. He could taste the red fruits and the hints of espresso and smell the subtle, earthy tones. The sommelier at the wine club had talked about the vintage's aroma, as though it contained half the species of a subtropical rainforest.

To Donovan, it tasted like vinegar.

Twelve weeks and three thousand bucks later, he still couldn't tell the difference between a cab and a chianti with his eyes closed. Or between a ten-dollar and two-hundred-dollar bottle.

He sipped again. Shrugged.

*Eh, good enough.*

In his lap, a double-spread ad invited Donovan to explore Inca life beyond Machu Picchu. He could hike Andean peaks, explore ancient ruins, and stroll along a nearly five-hundred-year-old stone path stretching from Chile to Colombia.

The pictures were certainly enticing. Pack llamas held up their heads proudly on the grasslands. Gray clouds threatened to storm into the gullies, turning streams into rivers. Wooden huts with thatched roofs nestled against stone walls, promising a good night's rest.

Adventures like these could be turned into impressive stories to share while sipping wine during intervals at the philharmonic.

Donovan turned the page and sipped his wine again. Adventure. *That's* what he thought he'd be doing now. Five years had passed since he'd sold his software company, converting half a decade of eighty-hour weeks into a single, eight-figure payment.

Now he didn't need to start the week with a stand-up meeting. There were no coding sprints to complete or marketing team meetings to hone a message and drive home a sales point.

Five years ago, he'd determined his life was his own again and he was going to travel. He'd see the world from Antarctica to Siberia. He'd cruise down the Danube and drink sangria in Spain, catch hairy crabs in Hangzhou and paddle up the Amazon.

The mansion he'd bought in Kentwood could stand empty until he and Pam returned exhausted, with their heads and camera folders filled with images and stories.

That'd been the plan, anyway.

So far, he'd gone no farther than Silicon Valley, minus the two-week vacation in Baja, California.

It was Pam's fault. Or maybe it was his.

He'd assumed once their bank account was brimming

with money, his wife would want to stop working as much as he did. It didn't occur to him she enjoyed her career and regarded clinical psychology as a calling.

Pam had no intention of giving up her work.

He could do what he wanted, but she would continue to see patients, conduct research, and teach classes at the local college.

Traveling would have to fit around her schedule.

But her schedule was full.

Instead of traveling, he'd picked up some hobbies.

The wine and cooking classes were fun. His role in designing the house and the garden cost him three interior designers and two landscapers, but he'd learned all about building codes and Tennessee's native coniferous trees.

He'd even developed a taste for classical music, was now a regular at concerts, and had started learning the piano.

His rendition of "Chopsticks" was coming along nicely.

Donovan closed the magazine. In front of him, the 135-inch flat screen of his home cinema stared blankly back. It was Sunday. Movie night. He'd picked a movie, an old Bourne thriller, and placed their weekly order—olives for her, pepperoni and pineapple for him.

But, of course, Pam had a deadline.

And the pizza was late.

The movie's opening image sat frozen on the Universal Studios logo.

"Pam!" he called through the open door. "Are you coming or what?"

"I'll be down in a minute." His wife's voice drifted back from her office upstairs. "Start without me."

Donovan sighed. He didn't want to start without her. He wanted to watch the movie *with* her. Was that too much to ask?

A bright, tinkling chime sounded out of the walls.

The pizza. About time. Fifteen minutes late. *But probably twenty minutes before Pam will be ending her workday. Maybe the food will bring her out of her office early.*

Donovan set his wine aside and left the theater room. He pressed the hallway intercom, bringing up the front door security feed.

There was the delivery guy, leaning out of his car window and grinning at the lens. He wasn't familiar, but Donovan buzzed open the gate and waited. The sound of crunching gravel grew louder, then changed to the softer pad of footsteps coming up the portico.

He opened the door to find the young man holding two pizza boxes in one hand. The pinky of his other hand was buried cuticle-deep in his left ear.

"It's about time." Donovan scowled. "And why did you take so long?"

Ignoring the first question, the delivery guy examined the results of his excavation and shrugged. "Finding your place is a bitch, man. The houses on this street are, like, three hundred miles apart."

Donovan wished the measurement was accurate. He often felt too close to his neighbors. But the distance between the properties, even if it wasn't as great as he would like, was certainly an asset. Privacy was one thing money struggled hardest to buy. He was proud he'd found a certain seclusion here, and so close to the city too.

He took the boxes and dropped a five-dollar bill into the pizza guy's hand, ignoring the kid's giant eye roll. Teens these days were so entitled. Why would he give a larger tip for late food?

"Don't be late next week." As Donovan kicked the door closed, he called up the stairs again. "Honey, the pizza's here. Why don't you finish tomorrow?"

"I'm coming." Silence. "Five minutes."

Five minutes meant twenty.

Donovan sighed and carried the boxes back to the cinema room. He wasn't going to wait. If Pam wanted to eat cold pizza, that was up to her. He would not ruin a perfectly good meal. And if she didn't want to watch the movie, well, her loss.

He slid the boxes onto the seat next to him, opened the lid, and reached for the remote control.

The tinkling chimes rang out again.

Irritation struck Donovan behind the eyes. "Kid must have forgotten something. Gonna take his tip back."

Donovan closed the pizza box and strode back to the front hallway. He yanked the door open.

"What the—"

The rest of his sentence died in his throat as he took in the person standing before him.

No, not a pizza delivery guy. A rabbit?

As Donovan's mind attempted to compute the stranger's presence, he noted the shabby black morning coat, black slacks, dull dress shoes, and white gloves. That was where all semblance of reality ended.

The stranger wore a rabbit head with soft, dusty fur. A crooked whisker curled down toward the bucked teeth. Long ears sprouted from the mask, making the man appear abnormally tall.

"Seriously, what the fu—"

The rabbit lifted a gun, pointing it at Donovan's face.

## 13

Hagen pulled his agency-issued Explorer up to the curb in front of Candice Diaz's residence. He missed his cherry red Corvette with a passion, but Slade had started tossing out keys to the fleet of vehicles. Hagen got the message.

The Deems' housekeeper lived a strikingly different life than her former employers. Two garbage cans stood at an angle on a broken sidewalk slab. The early morning breeze caught a candy wrapper and swept it down the street. Weeds peeked through the sparse grass of the apartment building.

Hagen turned off the engine and released his seat belt.

"Never thought these little rural towns would have streets as crappy as the city."

Chloe reached for the door handle. "You should get out into the country more often then, city boy. Plenty of poor people out here in the sticks."

He locked the vehicle with a *beep* of the fob and tested the handle. Surrounded by broken asphalt and low-slung electrical wires as they were, maybe it was best that he hadn't driven his car. It wouldn't have been more out of place if he'd parked it in the middle of a frozen lake.

Chloe laughed at his security efforts. "Don't worry about it. If someone wants to steal a federal vehicle, your little lock isn't going to stop them. Anyway, the apartment's right here."

Hagen pressed the lock button for the second time. The Explorer's lights flashed again as the *beep* went off.

Candice lived less than fifteen miles from her old boss's estate, but it might as well have been a different country.

"And to think, Stella and Ander got to go to the philharmonic this morning."

Chloe's eyebrows rose. "Jealous much?"

"Damn right. There's probably air-conditioning there. I guess I should be grateful we're not chasing down his mother-in-law's life, like Caleb and Martin."

"Not what I meant." Chloe arched her eyebrows, telling Hagen she knew he was dodging her question. "I was talking about you being jealous of Ander, and you know it." She stopped in the walkway to the apartment building, blocking his way. "What's the story with you and Stella?"

He had no idea how to answer that, so he played dumb. "Story?"

"C'mon, you don't have to have survived Quantico to see something's up between you two. I mean, Stella's cute. You're all right, I guess. Maybe a little workplace crush?"

Hagen gritted his teeth. *Why did everyone have to stick their noses into his affairs?* "There's nothing going on. We're just friends, okay? And colleagues."

Chloe lifted both hands in an *I won't push any further* gesture. That was always the good thing about Chloe. Put up a boundary, and she respected it. But she still held his gaze a bit longer than necessary, giving him time to say more.

He set his jaw. Chloe wasn't going to get any information from him.

"Okay. None of my business." She started toward the building's entrance. "But I'm going to tell you now. You hurt her, I'll hurt you a lot more."

*That* was unexpected. Stella, in a few short weeks, had managed to make friends in all the right places.

He followed Chloe to the building entrance. She scanned the names on the intercom and pressed the worn button beside C. ..*az*.

A buzz sounded from deep in the building, as loud and welcoming as an angry hive.

There was no reply.

Chloe tried again, pushing the button twice. After a moment, the door opened enough to reveal the round, irritated face of a woman in her forties. A strong jaw and sharp eyebrows gave her the look of a *luchadora*—one of the famed professional female Mexican wrestlers. Her black hair was piled up on her head in a tight bun, as though it were always in the way and needed strong taming.

Hagen attempted a smile, but it didn't make it very far. "Candice Diaz?"

The woman didn't open the door any wider. "*Sí*. Yes. If you've come for the dryer, you're too late. They took it already."

Hagen pulled out his ID. "I'm Hagen Yates. This is my colleague, Chloe Foster. We're with the FBI. We want to ask you some questions. Can we come in?"

"It's about Mr. Deem?"

Hagen nodded.

Candice passed a hand over her eyes. "I'll come out. Wait one minute."

Hagen put his ID away and leaned against the side of the building. After a few minutes, the door opened again, and she emerged. She tightened a fanny pack over a pair of black leggings that clung to her solid thighs. Her top was a loose, white t-shirt with a low neck.

Candice Diaz, Hagen decided, was a woman who dressed for comfort. Fashion was a distant second.

She tossed her head, causing her high bun to wobble, and started down the street. "Let's walk. My kid is with a friend, and I could use some exercise. And my place is a mess."

Hagen set off after her. "I'd have thought a housekeeper's home would be all sparkles and shine."

Candice grinned. It transformed her. She had the kind of smile that wiped away all the worries and troubles of life.

"Ha! Shows what you know. I'm a single mom. By the time I get back to *mijo*, I'm too tired to even look at a mop again. I crash on the sofa and let the mess build up. Eventually, I tidy everything, but today is not that day."

"At least you'll have more time now."

Chloe poked him in the rib cage. A bit too late, he understood the insensitivity of his comment.

Candice's smile vanished. Her face darkened, anger replacing her earlier ease.

"Time, sure. But money? Uh-uh. With the whole family… gone…" She crossed herself and sniffed hard. "No one is paying my wages. Jem already told me he won't need me for now. He said he'll be in touch when he's decided what to do with the house. Like I can wait that long. Twelve years and *pssht*." She snapped her fingers. "*Gone*…just like that."

Chloe's jaw clenched. Hagen knew if Jem stood in front of them right now, it would've taken all his persuasive skills and most of his strength to stop Chloe from kicking the guy in the head.

And he couldn't blame her. Maybe Ander was right. Maybe Jem was the dark soul they were looking for.

"That's…rough."

Candice waved away his concern with a flick of her wrist.

"I'm not surprised. That boy has given his family no shortage of trouble. Drugs and women and...oh, you name it. One thing I learned in twenty years of cleaning big houses. You can be as rich as you want in this world, but you can't buy your way out of asshole kids."

Chloe chuckled. "You can sure buy your way into them, though."

"Ha! Too true. The rest of us got nothing to give but love. And you can't go too far wrong with that."

Candice led them off the street to a path that ran through a small woodland.

"How was working for Jeremy Deem? And his wife?"

Candice shot him a glance as she picked up speed, holding her elbows above her waist.

"Oh, Mrs. Deem was nice enough. Always said hello and asked after my little Juan. Sometimes, after a party or a special dinner or something, she'd give me some of the leftover dessert for *mijo*. A slice of cake or some pudding or something. Charity. Made me feel like a human garbage can." She shrugged. "But my Juan didn't care, so how could I say no?"

"Right. What about her husband?"

Candice lengthened her stride.

Hagen stretched to keep up. Candice might have more than a decade on him, but she didn't lack stamina.

"I didn't have a whole lot to do with him. He wasn't usually home when I was there. Mostly, though, I thought he was a jerk. He was usually in his library when he was home, barking down the phone at someone. Mrs. Deem would ignore him when he was in one of those moods. Then she'd give whoever he'd shouted at a big tip. Only reason they'd come back."

Hagen dodged a washboarded section of the path. "Was there anyone the Deems were particularly close to? Any best friends?"

Candice shook her head. "Mrs. Deem, she was very private. She had a few friends she met for lunch sometimes. But they rarely came to the house. Mr. Deem was always seeing people, always going out. And she'd have to go with him, whether she wanted to or not."

"You don't think she wanted to go?"

"No. They'd go to these big special events. Charity things. She'd have to dress up, put on her jewels. She always hated it. People's eyes always on her. That's why that video was such a shock for her."

Hagen almost tripped over a tree root. Candice shot a disparaging look at his Oxfords. He ignored her silent rebuke. "What video?"

Candice finally slowed her long strides, stopping in the middle of the path. "You don't know about the video? It was maybe…three years ago. Mr. Deem rented some big, private plane to fly some of his biggest clients to Europe. I think he took some officials too. Some 'top people,' he said." She rolled her eyes, showing exactly what she thought of them.

"Why?"

She wrinkled her nose. "He'd arranged a private concert for them. Some famous musician. I don't know who, but the whole thing was a big deal. Mrs. Deem talked about it for weeks. The amount he was spending. And not just the plane and the music. He ordered lots of food for them, lots of wine." Candice's face creased with laughter. "Too much food and wine. And not enough time to recover from the flight. They all fell asleep at the concert."

The incident might have happened three years ago but remembering it made her laugh as though it had happened yesterday.

Hagen waited for her giggle fit to stop. "So what was the video?"

Candice lowered her hand from her mouth, but the smile lingered. "Sorry. Excuse me. So funny. One of the waiters filmed them. He put the video on YouTube or something. Millions of views. I think someone made a meme." She shrugged as if to say, *What can you do?*

"What was on the video?" Hagen had to temper his growing impatience.

"There they were, all these bigwigs in their suits and jewels, all sleeping away and snoring while the pianist played. Poor man couldn't see them. Mrs. Deem was horrified. She felt so bad for the pianist."

"What did Mr. Deem think?"

"He thought it was the funniest thing ever. Said the performance was terrible anyway. Something about pacing and lack of emotion." Candice shook her head and started back the way they'd come. "Juan will be home soon. I'd better get back."

## 14

Stella sat in the auditorium of the Kentwood Philharmonic and rubbed the back of her neck. Her earlier dream haunted her. Even though the audience seats were empty, she felt like someone was behind her. As soon as she lowered her hand, the tingle of being watched returned, running down her spine. She peered over her shoulder.

Apart from Ander's, all the seats in the theater were empty.

Still, Stella wished she was in the last row with a wall at her back instead of near the front row with nothing but empty space and darkness sneaking up on her.

Ander noticed her fidgeting. "You okay?"

"Yeah...yeah, I'm fine. Just the air-conditioning blowing down my neck. They lay it on strong here."

"We can move, if you want. Got the whole theater to choose from." He opened his arms wide, offering her any choice of seats.

"It's okay. Wouldn't want to disturb them." She nodded toward the stage.

The orchestra was already in place and tuning up for

rehearsal. Three cellists sat on the right of the stage, sending long, deep notes into the hall. Those growls were interrupted by short blasts from the trumpets and the reedy hum of clarinets. On the left, a cluster of violinists squeaked out bursts of notes that stopped suddenly before returning clearer and in tune.

The result was a discordant mix of sounds similar to an elementary school band concert.

It was the very opposite of a professional orchestra.

"Don't worry. They sound better when they're actually playing." A woman, who appeared to be in her mid-forties, with short, blond hair that swooped across one eye, made her way down the row toward them. Her purple satin blouse hung loose, but her black, knee-length skirt clung to her thighs.

Either the philharmonic was able to pay staff extremely well, or close relatives of the rich found jobs in places like this. It was also possible both were true. This woman's hair and clothing practically screamed wealth.

She extended her hand. "Amy Cooper. I'm the director. So sorry to keep y'all waiting."

Stella shook her hand, noting Amy Cooper's French manicure and glittering diamond ring. "Stella Knox, FBI. And this is my colleague, Ander Bennett."

Amy greeted Ander and took the seat next to Stella.

Stella shuffled uncomfortably. Holding an interview in a theater wasn't ideal, but they'd arrived to find the offices amid renovation. The walls were covered in plastic sheeting. Between the thumps of nail guns and the shrieks of the drills, a rehearsing orchestra was the quieter option.

Amy brushed the flap of blond hair away from her eye. "Wish y'all had come for the concert instead of the rehearsal. Oh, but wait now. Listen to this."

She gestured toward the stage.

A slight woman in a black, sleeveless t-shirt tucked into black jeans strode in front of the orchestra. Something in the way she moved reminded Stella of Chloe. She was young, probably in her early twenties.

Jet-black hair matched her clothes and her shoes. Her eyebrows were tapered, so they arced over the middle of her eye and ended in points as sharp as a new pencil. They could literally see the fine detail from their seats. Her chin was narrow. She paused and nodded at Amy.

As she approached the piano—though she didn't acknowledge the other performers—they gradually ceased their bow strokes and trumpet toots.

By the time she sat at the grand piano with stick-perfect posture, the auditorium was silent.

Stella was as transfixed as everyone else. The woman was striking.

Amy leaned closer. Stella could smell the director's morning macchiato on her breath. "Listen to this. She's going to play Ravel's *Pavane for a Dead Princess*. It's her favorite warm-up."

The woman held her hands over the keyboard. As her fingers drifted over the keys, the auditorium filled with the warmest, most exquisite sound Stella had ever heard.

There was no showmanship or demonstration of rapid finger work. A gentle, slow harmony expanded over the seats, turning the air into clouds of memories and images.

Stella's mind slipped away. She saw herself sitting at her brother's bedside, his gray fingers clasped in her hand. When she'd walked out of the hospital the day he died, the heat suffocated her. Her mind had been fogged, and her heart numbed. It felt as if the music was setting that long-buried cloud of pain finally free.

The pianist climbed octaves, and Stella pictured her mother at her kitchen table in Florida. Barbara Knox Rotenburg worried about her husband, fearful he would have another heart attack. Stella pictured her terror of being left alone. Her heart broke at the thought. When the musician slipped back into the piece's clear, subtle melody, a tear rose in Stella's eye.

As the pianist ceased playing and lifted her fingers from the keyboard, Stella saw a wet line also traced down Ander's cheek. She imagined he had been thinking about his son.

"Who is that?" Stella swallowed against the lump in her throat.

"That's Lisa Kerne." Amy dabbed at the corner of her eye. "Isn't she wonderful? She's going to go so far. It's in her genes, you see. Lisa was born with talent in spades." Amy tucked her tissue back into her pocket. "We've got about ten minutes before the conductor gets here, and the rehearsal starts in earnest. I understand you have some questions about Jeremy Deem. Such an awful thing. He was a great supporter of the orchestra, always ready to help."

The images and emotions Lisa Kerne had inspired faded.

Jeremy Deem. His murder. That was what mattered now.

Stella took a deep breath. "He was a generous donor, I believe."

Amy nodded reverently. "Oh, yes. Very generous. It's rare to find someone as dedicated as Jeremy was to the world of music. We would never have been able to afford these renovations if it wasn't for his support. We're so very grateful."

Ander rested an elbow on his knee, half twisting in his seat to better see Amy. With his curls hanging past his cheek, he looked like an art critic explaining the importance of Wagner's *Ring Cycle*.

"You sure it was only the arts he pursued here? I understand he also turned many of your supporters into his clients."

Amy's jaw tightened, and a steeliness came into her eyes.

"If Jeremy used his support to meet like-minded people who also *happened* to be in need of his company's services, that was none of the philharmonic's business. And frankly, Agent, I'd be surprised if it's any of yours."

Amy's belligerence amused Stella. As a music director, Amy knew nothing of the business of tracking down killers and following leads. "If it's connected to Jeremy Deem, it's our business. Did anyone mind him using intermissions to talk business? Or board meetings to promote his fund? He made no enemies here?"

Ander leaned closer. "Or rivals?"

Amy shook her head sharply, sending the artful lock of blond hair back across her eye. "On the *contrary*. Jeremy Deem was very popular with all our supporters. And with the musicians too. He not only donated generously to support the orchestra, he also sponsored private concerts. He would often hire up-and-coming performers, as well as established names, to play for him on special occasions."

Stella frowned. "Is that generous? Sounds like he was hiring musicians for his corporate events."

Amy folded her fingers in her lap and offered a tight-lipped smile. If she was trying to show she could be patient in the most trying of circumstances, she was failing…in the least trying of circumstances.

"Engagements like these are vital for musicians. Not everyone can be a great soloist like Lisa Kerne. By organizing and paying for private concerts, Jeremy enabled young musicians to earn a living from their art and make vital connections."

Deem was also getting a private performance that would impress his client. It was a power play. If he'd wanted to support the arts, he could have paid for public performances anyone could hear. But Stella didn't point this out.

Ander leaned closer. "Do you know which musicians he—?"

Before he could complete his question, a man strode onto the stage. His wiry gray hair stretched past his ears, and he held a conductor's baton in his hand. He tapped twice on the top of a music stand, and the musicians picked up their instruments and fell silent.

"Let's see what you've got today!" He lifted the baton. As he lowered it, the drums and violins burst into life.

Then, electronic and disjointed, a woman's voice rose from beside Stella, singing of her love of rock and roll and calling for another dime to be placed in the jukebox, baby.

Stella froze.

The violins and drums stopped.

The conductor turned and stared at them.

Beside her, Ander scrabbled in his pocket for his phone.

"Sorry," he mumbled as he killed his ringtone and took the call.

He listened for a moment. By the time he hung up, the color had drained from his cheeks.

"We have to go. They've found another victim."

## 15

Stella heard the shouting before she reached the police tape blocking Donovan Freeman's house. A woman's loud voice left little room for anyone to throw a word back.

Ander trudged up the gravel drive beside Stella. "Someone's not happy."

"Should they be?"

"Nope. But so much for letting the dead rest in peace."

The house was one of the largest Stella had ever seen, bigger than the Deems' mansion. A pair of newly painted Greek-style pillars supported the wide portico. One wing of the house disappeared along the rolling lawn to Stella's right. To her left, a long set of windows morphed into a garage wide enough to hold at least five cars side by side.

Ander appraised the tall windows on the second floor, then glanced over his shoulder at the iron entrance gate. "I should get me one of these."

Stella scoffed. "Right after you win the lottery."

"Got my ticket. Fifty million this week. Cross your fingers for me."

"And my toes."

The shouting stopped. Then started again.

"But if you win, I'm taking fifty percent."

"As long as you can prove it was your fingers and toes that did it, deal."

Stella knew she would never live in a house like this, and neither would Ander. The best they could hope for was retiring in a condo near a lake. And retirement felt a long way away.

A Kentwood police officer stood guard at the doorway. The acne on his chin suggested he was barely out of high school. He shuffled his feet as the woman's voice rose again.

Stella and Ander pulled out their badges.

He barely glanced at the IDs before asking them to sign the crime scene logbook. Once they had, he handed them the dreaded forensic suits.

"You'll need to put these on. Forensics is inside with a couple corpses." He cupped a hand to the side of his mouth. "And Chief Gray sounds like she's aiming to make a couple more."

"That's Chief Gray?" Stella had a hard time picturing the political animal she'd met at the Deems' mansion shouting. But she understood people changed under pressure.

Stella and Ander took the suits and slipped them on. As they pulled up their hoods and tugged on their gloves, the chief's volume increased.

The officer leaned closer and whispered, "Good luck."

Stella bent under the tape and pushed open the door. The scene was horribly familiar.

A large, marble-tiled foyer opened to a living room. An open pizza box lay empty in the middle of a coffee table between two overstuffed sofas.

Beyond that was a grand piano. The instrument wasn't as large as the one in the Deems' house. Maybe it was a baby grand. Its location at the far end of the room suggested a certain hesitancy about its presence, as though the owner was worried someone might ask him to play it.

Two club chairs faced the piano. Their occupants sat unnaturally stiff in their seats, rigor mortis having taken a solid hold of their muscles.

Stella and Ander approached the scene with caution.

The woman sat farthest from the piano, her neck bent toward her shoulder. Like Penny Deem, she had a hole above one eye and a thick line of blood down her cheek.

Next to her, the male victim seemed to be examining the ceiling. The backward tilt of his head exposed the blood-soaked t-shirt and stretched open the deep cut running around his throat.

Even from ten feet away, Stella saw the pink muscle on the underside of the slit. There was even a small patch of white, which she assumed was bone.

The killer was growing more forceful. Either he was becoming angrier or more confident in using his weapons.

Neither was a good sign.

Stella's stomach tightened. Since joining the FBI, she'd faced the most savage of serial killings. And while the sight of blood never moved her, seeing the pain a victim had suffered always tore a hole in her gut. Another person lost. Another family dropped into mourning.

"This is exactly what I was trying to avoid! The last thing this town needs is more dead residents."

Stella spun around. Two people, covered head to toe in Tyvek suits, stood near the base of a large, sweeping staircase.

Even with their hoods up and masks on, Stella recognized Slade and Chief Gray. The chief's cheeks above her mask were bright red.

She jabbed a blue-gloved finger toward Slade's chest. "Do you have any idea how much these people pay in city taxes?

Christ, if they leave, if they stop paying, and God help us, if they sue. Do you have any idea how much your incompetence is hurting my department? How much your inability to catch this murderer is hurting *me*?"

Slade practically vibrated with an anger Stella could feel.

There were times when a hardness would come into the SSA's face, and the target of his steely gaze would fall silent. As long as Slade held their gaze, with his forehead creased and his jaw set, they could do nothing but wait quietly.

That hardness dropped onto Chief Gray like a physical weight. She stopped shouting. Her voice faded. She seemed to shrink into her suit.

After several seconds, Slade finally spoke. "Let me remind you, Chief, that *you* called *us* to help. If you no longer require that assistance, if you think you can manage this on your own, you're more than welcome. My team is overworked, understaffed, and long overdue for some time off. I'll have no truck with helping people who don't want help. Leaving you and your young squad to hunt down this serial killer is fine by me. You can explain to your local taxpayers why their neighbors keep dying. You just let me know."

Chief Gray stepped back. "No, of course. You understand…this has all been very—"

Slade turned on his heel, addressing Stella and Ander without even looking their way. "With me. Hagen and Chloe should be here shortly."

"We're here."

Two more Tyvek-bedecked agents stood in the front entrance.

"Follow me."

They trudged behind him down the hallway off the living room. Their booties slid against the marble floor until they reached the first room on the right.

Mac sat at a large desk, a laptop open before her. She

offered a bright smile that contrasted with the bruises on her face and the grim surroundings.

Slade lowered his hood and pulled down his mask.

"Close the door."

Ander closed the door behind him. He and Stella lowered their own masks. Slade tapped a gloved finger on the desk.

"That woman is driving me nuts. But she's not wrong. We started this case with three victims. Now we've got five. I think we all know our unsub won't stop there. And we're not much further in this investigation than we were yesterday. I know you're all tired. I know you've all—*we've* all—been through a lot recently. But we need to focus and *get this done*."

He slammed his hand onto the surface of the desk.

Stella swallowed. She'd never seen Slade lose his cool before. But perhaps she should have expected it. Over the last few weeks, he'd seen a team member shot, led an investigation into the murders of teenage girls the same age as his daughters, then hunted a serial killer who'd kidnapped two members of his team.

Slade flicked a finger in front of the monitor. "Show them what you've got. I'd better talk to the chief again. See if she's calmed down."

As Slade left the room, Mac clicked a button on the keyboard. The other four agents circled around her.

The video started running. A car drew up in front of the door, the blue and red triangle on the roof advertising fresh, hot pizza. The door opened, and the delivery guy stood at the door, handed over the pizza, and drove away.

Mac moved the video on. "I think we can rule him out. He clearly leaves the front gate. But...here."

A few minutes after the delivery guy disappeared, another figure approached the door. The new arrival wore a long morning coat and white gloves. A large rabbit mask hid his face.

He rang the doorbell. As soon as the door opened, he pulled a gun.

Ander exhaled a long breath. "That's our guy."

Mac hit pause, framing the strange mask on the screen. "Why do these people never check their cameras if they're going to go through all the trouble of *having* them?"

"He probably thought the pizza guy forgot something." But Stella understood Mac's point. To Stella, he looked like a grainy ghost straight out of a horror movie. Why on earth would you open the door to *that*?

Chloe chuckled. "Let's hope that's our guy…singular. If we've got two killer rabbits now, we'll have four next week."

Stella ignored her. They had two bodies next door. This wasn't the time for levity. "What do we know about the victims?"

Mac took the briefing lead. "Here's what I've got. Donovan's a gazillionaire or thereabouts. He made a fortune in software a few years back. His company went for a couple hundred million, and he walked away with over fifty."

Ander made a low whistle. "Nice. Knew I was in the wrong business."

Mac continued. "But get this. A few years ago, he began sponsoring the philharmonic, and whaddaya know, Jeremy Deem started looking after his money."

Frustration at their lack of progress melted away. They were getting somewhere. "We've got a link. Maybe we can get ahead of our mad bunny. There's a pretty good chance his next victim will also be a client, a local, or both."

Chloe chewed her bottom lip. "Yeah, but Jeremy Deem had over a hundred clients."

Mac leaned back in her chair, as if she wanted to put some distance between herself and the information the computer offered. "And most of them live in Kentwood."

"But how many own a piano?" Stella ventured.

## 16

Hagen pulled up his hood. "Right. How many own a piano? That's one of about a hundred questions we need to be focused on right now." He thought of the video Candace Diaz had mentioned earlier and filed a mental note to locate it. "I'll break the news to Chief Gray. I'm sure she'll be thrilled to hear dozens of Kentwood citizens are potentially in our unsub's sights."

He slipped past Stella and out of the room. When he reached the end of the corridor, he found the living room empty except for a single forensic tech bagging the pizza box. Even the bodies were gone.

The tech didn't even lift her head as she spoke. "You looking for your boss?"

Hagen nodded. "Yeah."

"Out the front. The coroner just picked up the stiffs. Think the chief was getting green around the gills with those two sitting in here. Can't blame her, to be honest. And we've still got bits of blood and brain splattered on the floor. We'll have maggots crawling around here in no time."

Hagen shuddered. *Maggots in brain juice, jeez.*

"Thanks for that." He strode out of the house without looking back.

Chief Gray sat on the steps under the portico. She'd removed her Tyvek hood, and her gloves were balled in her hand.

Slade stood in front of her. He'd taken off bits of his forensic gear too. He looked up as Hagen came out of the house.

"Got anything?"

Hagen tugged at the Velcro on his suit. Even in the heat of the late morning, the air felt fresh out of the gear.

"Yeah, maybe. Mac's found a link between Freeman and Deem. It seems Freeman bought a subscription to the philharmonic recently. Deem was also managing his millions."

"You think someone is going after Deem and his clients?"

"That's the only link we've got so far, except for the fact they both live, lived, in Kentwood. That's the good news."

"What's the bad news?"

"Hundreds of people live in Kentwood, and a good percentage of them place their money with Jeremy Deem."

"Damn." Chief Gray propped her elbows on her knees and rolled the gloves between her hands. "Have you any idea at all who might be doing this?"

Hagen shook his head. "Nope. None."

Slade glared at him.

Hagen swallowed and adjusted his tone. "We're getting there. The links are coming together. We need to follow a few more threads. Chloe and I spoke to the Deems' housekeeper this morning. She mentioned something about a video. Maybe there's something there. We'll track it down. In the meantime, you can protect the people of Kentwood. I'll have Mac pull together a list of Deem's Kentwood clients. They should be warned."

The chief lifted her head. The thought of being able to do

something, or at least to be seen doing something, appeared to refresh her.

"Will do. And I'll set up regular patrols in the area. Check security cameras. Dammit, nothing is going to get in or out of this neighborhood without being seen and recorded. Not even a mouse."

Hagen couldn't help himself. "Or a rabbit."

Slade's glare grew darker. He opened his mouth to speak, but before he could begin, his phone rang. He took the call and walked up the gravel drive, listening carefully.

After a minute or two, he came back, shoving his phone into his pocket. A glimmer of satisfaction on his face sent a ripple of worry through Hagen. This would not be good.

"Got a job for you, Hagen."

Hagen licked his lips. He worried Slade had just figured out payback for Hagen's smart-assery.

"Kinda working on the video the housekeeper directed us to, Boss. I think there might be something there. We should certainly check it out."

"You can leave that to Mac. If it's online, she'll know how to find it. The medical examiner has everything set up for the autopsies. Impressively quick, that one." He paused and smiled—a little evilly, in Hagen's opinion. "I want you and Chloe to head down to the forensic center and take a closer look at the bodies."

## 17

My stomach grumbled, rattling against my rib cage. I felt as if I hadn't eaten a morsel in days, though last night I'd had…pizza.

That was the problem with the *nouveau riche*. No class. They clung to their old, middle-class culture. Maybe Donovan Freeman thought he was hip and happening by eating delivered pizza in his mansion on his shiny marble floors, but all it showed was his lack of taste. The man could've ordered anything he wanted from any restaurant in the area. He could fly in fresh lobster from Maine and hire a chef to prepare it for him, and he'd ordered pizza.

It was as if I, with all my skills and training, chose to play "Twinkle, Twinkle Little Star."

Unlike Freeman, Jeremy Deem had known how to eat. He'd hired a cook and had a whole, proper meal laid out. Real silver. Cloth napkins. That was how a man was supposed to live.

"Might as well have gotten a burger and fries. Some people wouldn't know culture if it sprouted in their armpits."

I was starving. Usually, I didn't have much of an appetite.

Coffee and bacon for breakfast would normally last the day. But only if I got a proper dinner.

And I expected a multimillionaire to provide better.

I glanced around my motel room, looking for anything to distract me from my rumbling belly.

The rabbit's eyes stared up from the pillow beside me. A couple spots of blood stained the edge of the right eyehole. Big, empty, see-through mesh. They couldn't see anything, those eyes.

I slipped it on. Lying on the motel bed, I could see straight through to the water-stained ceiling above. I could even make out the smears of three mosquitoes splattered next to the lamp.

All of that through an empty pair of eyes.

I tried to straighten one of the whiskers. But no matter how much I pulled, the thing would just spring back.

Didn't matter in the long run, I supposed. With a gun in my hand, I doubted anyone noticed what I wore. Which was a shame. I'd have liked them to have paid more attention. This rabbit face meant something to me. Always had.

A particularly large growl shook my guts. I needed sustenance.

I slipped the rabbit mask onto the floor and swung my legs to the ground. Then I grabbed my keys and was out the door.

I drove my old Nissan Maxima into the center of Kentwood.

The place gave me the shivers. In truth, I never liked to be too far from my motel room. There was always a chance someone would find my things while I was gone. Discover my mask. Pick up the wire I'd hidden between the mattress, now gritty with extra spots of blood.

But the town itself was small. Downtown, if it could be called that, held a single long strip mall with a few clothing stores, a single toy store, a shuttered home furnishing boutique, some kind of posh ice cream parlor, a couple sandwich places, and one music store.

Only one miserable music store in the whole town.

May as well close the whole world up and toss it into the sun.

I grabbed myself a sandwich from one of the shops. Then I headed to the little park behind the school across the street, where I found a bench to sit on while I ate.

The meal was nothing fancy, but it was better than pizza. Pear and brie on ciabatta. At least the sandwich shop was trying.

My patrons and sponsors used to take me to the most delightful places. Escargot in a Michelin-starred Parisian restaurant. Wagyu beef in a secret Tokyo diner. I once ate goulash on a golden plate in a luxury Budapest hotel.

And now here I was. Eating a just-above-mediocre sandwich on a bench in an almost empty park—alone.

Alone? Not entirely true.

There were others in the park. People like me with nothing to do but hang outside in the midday sun.

One of the park's visitors stood out. He'd placed an electric keyboard in the shade of a tree, attached it to a speaker, and was torturing the keys, banging and clanging.

A small crowd gathered in front of him as he performed. Why they didn't run screaming from the park with their hands over their ears, I didn't know.

Technically? It was competent enough, I supposed. But how could he go wrong with *show tunes*? I shuddered.

*"The Sound of Music." "Chicago." ...Is that something from* Cats?

And the audience loved it. They sang, and they swayed. Two turned pirouettes as though they were at the Bolshoi.

So much enthusiasm and excitement and movement for such god-awful excuses for music.

Good lord, I wanted to take his keyboard and beat him and his idiotic audience over the head with it. What a waste.

He could have played anything.

Prokofiev, Liszt, Beethoven...wonderful Beethoven. But no. We got Rodgers and Hammerstein and Andrew Lloyd Freaking Webber. And they loved it.

I threw half my sandwich into the bin and stormed out of the park.

Philistines. All of them. The world would be better off if they all met my piano wire.

## 18

Stella stood by the gate at the entrance to Donovan Freeman's house and took in the front garden. A wide flowerbed curved around the edge of the lawn, the creeping junipers sneaking between beds of zinnias and bursts of peonies. The graveled drive led up to the garage, then branched away in front of the portico, allowing guests to park their Porsches and Teslas directly in front of the house.

She examined the ground at the foot of the ten-foot brick wall dividing the property from the road.

"Guess this place will be on the market now. Maybe the murders will drive down the property value." Ander stood on the other side of the drive, eyeing the top of the wall, looking for any signs the killer had climbed over. "You'll come by after I move in?"

Stella straightened. There were no footprints here and no sign anyone had broken in. "Sure. But only after you've soaked the blood out of the floor."

"Aw, Stella. That's what I was inviting you over for."

"Then ask Hagen. He's more house-trained than me."

Ander's phone rang, his device's love of rock and roll taking Stella back to the awkward moment at the philharmonic. The corners of her lips raised in a smile.

He reddened again and strode up the side of the grass to take the call. After a few minutes, he came back, walking quickly.

"That was one of Chief Gray's men. She sent him to talk to the pizza delivery guy. The guy swears he didn't see anything or anyone. Not on the way here, not while he was here, and not when he left."

"Huh. That's strange."

"Yeah, but how did the pizza guy not see anything? There are only a few minutes between him leaving and Bugs Bunny arriving."

"He didn't look too observant, did he?" Stella cast her eye over the metal gate. The ironwork ended in long spears, ready to impale an intruder. "He seemed more interested in the contents of his ear than what was happening around him. If the killer snuck in behind him in the darkness when the gate opened, I'm not sure he'd have noticed."

"That would work. He could have been hiding somewhere outside, waiting for his opportunity."

Stella's phone pinged.

Mac had texted a message. *Here's the video the housekeeper was talking about.* A link was attached.

Ander stuck his hands into his pockets, waiting as she read the screen. "Let me guess. It's the pizza guy, and he remembers everything after all."

"No. It's Mac. She found the video. Here, she sent us something."

She touched the link as Ander came and stood behind her. The video app opened to reveal a clip lasting just under two minutes.

Ander read the video title. *"Boris the Boringest Plays Chopin's Nocturne, op. 9, no. 2.* Well, this should be a fun movie."

"Three-and-a-half million views." Stella's eyebrows rose. "Can't be too boring. Let's see what we've got."

She hit play.

A gentle tinkle of piano music came through her speakers. More classical. Yay.

Stella had never heard the piece before and didn't know whether she was listening to a genius play, but the pianist was clearly careful and proficient, if a little slow. Stella found the music deeply relaxing, as though the notes alone were thick enough to blanket the house and hide the destruction around her.

The tension in her shoulders eased. She leaned back until her shoulder touched Ander's chest. She immediately propped herself forward again, but she willed herself to keep her eyes open and her attention on the screen.

Ander leaned closer until his chest just touched Stella's shoulder again. "I wouldn't say he's boring. Just a bit…tame."

The pianist sat with his back to the audience. His hands drifted up and down in the light, his fingers caressing the keys.

The camera shifted to the right as the photographer moved, revealing a bit of the pianist's profile lit by a bright spotlight. His eyes focused on his fingers, his expression intent. For a slow piece, he was clearly exerting a great deal of mental effort, his playing demanding all his attention. As one note drifted away, he lifted his fingers and gently landed them on the keys of the next chord, pressing with only the lightest of force.

Stella leaned forward slightly. "No, you're wrong. He *is* boring."

A rasp sounded from somewhere to the left, quickly followed by a burst of laughter from behind the lens. The pianist didn't react. He seemed to be in his own world, swallowed by his music.

The camera panned to reveal some members of the audience. It was small, only a couple of dozen people from what Stella could tell from a quick count of the backs of their heads. Each member was seated on an ornate chair in a ballroom of what appeared to be a European hotel. Apart from the spotlight on the musician, the room was dark, but the gleam from that single light illuminated a patch of wall with gold rococo finishing.

As the camera moved from behind the audience and up the aisle, Stella saw the problem. "Oh, no. Look."

They were asleep. Some dozed with their heads tilted back. Others dropped their chins against the tops of their chests. One man in the front row had even twisted to the side, one leg wrapped over the other to recreate something close to the fetal position. As they snoozed in the shadows behind the pianist's back, the music lulled on.

She would have thought they were dead, except the pianist was still playing, and the director of this little show kept filming.

Pity dropped through Stella's chest, deep and heavy.

All the effort the pianist was putting in, all that work and training and concentration…and his entire audience had drifted off to dreamland.

A loud snorting rasped through the video. The camera jerked to the side to reveal a man in the front row drooling, his nose buzzing like an annoying fly.

"That's Jeremy Deem." Stella pointed at the sleeping man. His head lolled to one side, and, despite being partially hidden in the darkness, she could see his face. His mouth was open, and a thin line of drool created a dark stain on his shoulder. He was clearly the man from the first crime scene.

Laughter came from behind the lens again. It ended as abruptly as the video. The screen went black.

Ander whistled. "You're right. Rewind." Stella took the video back a few seconds. "And that must be Penny next to him."

A woman's arm was barely visible next to Jeremy Deem. A floral dress frilled around her shoulders. The graying curls were darker than the body they'd found in the Deems' house, but it was Penny Deem all right. Her neck was bent at an angle, and her chest rose and fell with the rhythm of deep sleep.

"Uh-oh. And there." Ander pointed to a figure two rows behind Jeremy Deem.

The man's face was mostly hidden in darkness, but it, too, was unmistakable. The same thin, gray hair. The same square jaw and short, upturned nose. Donovan Freeman's eyes were closed but his mouth was half open.

Stella turned the stud in her ear. "So we've got another link. Jeremy Deem. Kentwood. And this video. We need to identify and speak to the pianist right away."

"Right."

Stella cursed as the video stopped before she could get a good view of anyone else's face. "We need to know everyone in that audience."

Ander pulled out his phone. "I'll call Deem's assistant right now."

As he spoke, Stella scrolled down the page with her thumb. Beneath the video were over three hundred comments. Most were comprised of little more than laughing emojis, interspersed with *LOL* and rows of smileys.

One commenter, though, had been busier than most.

Alice20. *Shame on you for filming this, and shame on*

*everyone in the audience who's sleeping. I hope you all die and burn in hell.*

Beneath the laughing smiles and crying faces, Alice20 had repeatedly written *evil bitch* and *hope you die*.

She showed Ander the screen. "Let's also see if Mac can find out who Alice20 is."

## 19

Hagen wished he'd been nicer to Chief Gray. He should have told her she was doing a great job—the fine folks of Kentwood were lucky to have her. Thanks to her, they'd find the killer in no time!

And he should have said it all in front of Slade.

Maybe if he hadn't been such a smart-ass, he'd be at the Freemans' house, checking the grounds and talking with Stella.

And maybe Ander would have been in the morgue, standing in front of the naked corpse of Jeremy Deem.

Medical Examiner Casper Brennan tapped at his computer.

Hagen hated these places. It wasn't only the chemical smell, though the caustic mix of death and ammonia burned the back of his throat and made his skin itch.

The sight of the bodies, naked and on a clean slab, always struck him like a slap with a wet towel.

They were so…bare.

At a crime scene, bodies were victims. Whether they'd been killed in their own homes or stabbed on the street,

Hagen could see how they'd lived, where they went, and even how they thought. Every crime scene held a thousand different fragments of a life he could absorb and understand.

A morgue stripped an individual to their barest essentials.

Looking down at the mortuary slab, Hagen couldn't know whether Jeremy Deem was rich or poor, married or single, enjoyed classical music or hard rock. His body was gray. His arms lay unnaturally straight at his sides. The fuzz of white hair above his pecs should have been hidden beneath a custom-fitted shirt.

And as he stood over Deem's corpse, Hagen couldn't help but know this was how his own father had ended up—naked and exposed to prying eyes. He couldn't imagine it.

The last time Hagen had seen his dad was when he'd left for work that fateful morning. Seth Yates had been wearing his dark suit and shiny brown shoes. Sometime between the front door and his funeral, his father would have been stripped and laid out like this. And a law enforcement officer like Hagen would have stood over the slab and wondered how he'd lived and how he'd died.

Seth Yates's story still wasn't resolved.

Chloe, who looked as out of place to Hagen in her all-black ensemble, tilted her head. "Guess we don't have to wonder about the cause of death for this one."

The medical examiner answered without lifting his head or slowing his keyboard clicking. "Nope. Cause of death was asphyxiation due to ligature strangulation."

"Oh, not loss of blood then?" Hagen laughed in spite of himself. Apparently, they *should* wonder about the cause of death.

Chloe's glare was less effective when her lips curled into a smile.

Brennan hit save and turned around. He was in his mid-fifties with receding blond hair. He shoved his hands into the pockets of his white coat.

"No, no. The crushing of the windpipe would have cut off the supply of oxygen to the brain first. The loss of blood would have helped, of course, and would likely have hastened his death. But in these cases, strangulation usually does the job rather quickly."

Hagen swayed at the casual description of death. His knees softened. He touched the edge of the slab, if only to feel something solid through his latex gloves.

When he'd joined law enforcement, he'd assumed the sight of blood and guts and twisted bodies would leave him unmoved, like looking at a gutted deer.

It never did.

Sometimes he suspected his body was telling him something his head refused to believe— violence wasn't his world, and he should leave it all behind.

His body could shut the hell up.

The medical examiner stepped forward as if to defend the metallic gurneys. "Please don't touch. The body leaves all kinds of fluids on there. And please put on fresh gloves." Brennan didn't give Hagen much of an option. He pulled a new set out of the box hanging on the wall.

Hagen accepted the gloves. "Anything else you can tell us?"

"Not much. Almost nothing in the stomach. The other victims managed to take a bite or two of their dinner before they were interrupted. Here."

Back at his desk, he brought up an image on his computer monitor. The picture showed the contents of a stomach, a small amount of mash dotted with green at the bottom of a dark, fleshy hole.

A wave of nausea hit Hagen. He swallowed to keep his own lunch down.

"What is that?"

"Salmon and asparagus. In Penny Deem's stomach."

Chloe didn't appear affected by the sight of partially digested fish and veggies. She leaned forward to take a closer look. "Did you find anything in the food?"

"No. We'll need to wait on the tox screen, but upon physical examination, I could detect nothing unusual in any of the victims' stomachs and no wounds other than some light bruising around the arms where they were bound. Apart from the wounds that caused their deaths, of course."

Chloe left the computer and leaned over Deem's body, examining the rip in Jeremy Deem's throat up close. "So strangulation for this victim and gunshots for the other two. And you're sure?"

Brennan rested the small of his back against his desk and crossed his ankles. He seemed comfortable by the wall, as though the corpse dominating the room no longer held any interest for him.

"What else did you have in mind, Agent? Shark attack? It's all simple and straightforward."

Chloe didn't respond immediately. Her face remained placid as she scanned the torn edges of Jeremy Deem's neck.

Hagen frowned. "This isn't simple at all. Garroting is a nasty way to go, and not something we see very often, even in the FBI."

The medical examiner pulled on a new set of gloves. "True. I suppose I should thank you two for bringing me this one. I haven't seen a killing like this for…ooh, it must be twenty years now. An old-style gangland revenge killing. Killer tended to use cheese wire then, but I don't think that's the case here due to the larger wire gauge. Look."

He tilted Jeremy Deem's head back. The gash across the throat widened until it stretched more than an inch from edge to edge, revealing pink muscle and glimpses of white bone. Hagen closed his eyes and gritted his teeth. The wound reappeared, emblazoned on the inside of his eyelids. He inhaled deeply.

*Think of something else. Think of a run in the park. Fresh air. Stella.*

Imagining Stella made him feel better, stronger, more confident. The vision of her assured him he could do this.

He ignored the nausea. His legs rediscovered their strength and balance. He opened his eyes.

*Yuck.*

Chloe leaned over the corpse to get a better view.

Brennan had one gloved finger on the bottom edge of the wound. "Do you see how the bruising here is both deep and wide? The wire must have been thicker than cheese wire. Maybe an electric guitar string. But I'd lean more toward piano wire. Here. Look at this one."

He removed his finger from Jeremy Deem's throat and released his temple. Deem's head flopped down, narrowing the gash.

Brennan rolled Donovan Freeman's body out from a corner of the room. The medical examiner dragged the cart toward Hagen and Chloe. "This is the new one. Fresh as a daisy. I haven't started on him yet, but you can see the wound. Same angle around the neck, similar depth of incision, and similar bruising around the cut itself."

Hagen glanced at the ceiling instead of the corpses. "And you think the wound is consistent with the use of piano wire?"

"Well, there may be more options. Piano wire is the most likely, I'd say."

Chloe examined the wound. "Thank you. All the victims were found seated in front of a piano, so piano wire is not a bad theory."

Hagen nodded, seizing on the idea. "Maybe he took the

wire from the piano itself. We should get back to the Deems' house and check. It might be missing a string."

Chloe nodded. "Good idea. Let's—"

But Hagen was already halfway across the room and headed for the door.

## 20

Stella and Ander headed to Mac's office when they got back to the resident agency.

When she opened the office door, Stella found the cyber expert with her arms folded on her desk, her back straight, and her lips drawn into a thin line. Mac looked like the smartest kid in the class, about to receive a commendation from the teacher for writing an exceptionally good essay.

Stella eyed her friend. "You're looking very pleased with yourself."

Ander plopped into the seat opposite Mac and let the chair swivel. "If you've bagged yourself the last protein bar in the vending machine, I will not be happy."

Mac pulled a sad face. The bandage on her temple stretched. The bruise above her brow made her fake sadness appear particularly pathetic, adding to the dramatics. "No, I've done something even better than emptying the vending machine."

Stella crossed her fingers. "You've found our pianist?"

They'd been trying to locate Boris the Boringest for hours now, but the musician seemed to have dropped off the planet. Even the check Jeremy Deem's firm had written for the pianist's time had been linked to a business account... Boris Entertainment.

They were also trying to track down each of the audience members, but Jeremy Deem's assistant claimed she wasn't the one who'd made those arrangements. The trip had been planned by the Budapest Philharmonic Orchestra, and Karen Neuglass had been happy to leave all the details to their administrative department.

Mac wrinkled her nose. "I'm good, but not that good. But while tech has been working to clear up the video enough to recognize the audience members, I've tracked down your Alice20."

"That's some fast work." Guilt settled in Stella's stomach. She should've insisted Mac go home rather than dive into a big research project.

Ander didn't appear to share Stella's remorse. He rocked his chair first one way, then the other. "How did you do it? Did you have to dig into the back end of the internet? Hack into servers? Or slip the FBI's latest, greatest spyware into the side of someone's laptop when they weren't looking?"

Mac laughed. "I did an internet search. Took me about ten minutes. Here, look."

She swung one of the monitors on her desk around and wheeled her own chair to the end, joining Ander and Stella.

The screen showed the video of *Boris the Boringest*. The image was frozen on Jeremy Deem's open mouth. Mac must have stopped the playback mid-snore.

Mac scrolled down the screen. Their victim disappeared, replaced by a list of names and emojis. Mac slipped the cursor onto Alice20 and clicked. The screen switched to a page showing an avatar with a large capital A, a list of videos, and a tab for Alice20's favorite channels, but little else.

"If you tap Alice20's name, you get her profile. There's

not much here. She hasn't filled in any of the profile fields or uploaded videos of her own, but you can see what other channels she watches."

Stella scanned the channels. "It's all classical music."

"Right. She hasn't got the most varied of tastes."

Ander pushed his chair against the wall and stretched out his long legs. "So she's a classical music fan. We could've guessed that from her reaction."

Mac clicked an open tab on her browser. The screen changed to show a forum.

"Yeah, but her singular interest got me thinking. I started searching classical music forums for her username. We got lucky. If she'd chosen something common like Jane Smith, we'd have struggled. But Alice20 is unusual enough. I hit this."

She clicked over to a page where music fans were holding a discussion about the best recording of Grieg's Piano Concerto in A Minor.

Ander scooted toward the screen. "Wow. I've always wondered about Grieg."

Mac chuckled. "Then you and Alice20 should get on well because she thinks it's the Leif Ove Andsnes recording from—"

Stella cut in. "Mac, where are you going with this?"

Mac paused and gave Stella a teasing, superior glance. "You know. Most of my work involves running specialized software that decrypts hard drives, burrows into servers, and reconstructs data. I can't tell you guys what I do because there're maybe a few hundred people in the country who understand it. But this I can explain. Now, listen."

There was something heartwarming about watching her friend explain how she'd solved a mystery in almost no time at all. Not once did Mac touch the bandage on the side of her head or rub the back of a neck that still had to be sore.

Mac waved a hand. "I found the album on Amazon, and Alice20 has reviewed it."

She clicked another tab, bringing up the review page for a piece of music Stella had never heard of, played by a musician whose name she couldn't pronounce.

Without thinking, Stella began reading Alice20's review aloud. "*'Andsnes's playing reveals a remarkable passion rare among contemporary pianists.'* That's nice."

Ander continued reading over Stella's shoulder. "*'His precision and balance are almost unique. To hear the delicacy of his technique combined with his feel for the sonata's cadences makes for a very special treat.'*" He snorted. "Alice20 should try pistachio ice cream. Now that's a very special treat."

"Well, she's not threatening to garrote the musician, so I guess that's a plus."

Mac tapped the screen, bringing their attention back to the matter at hand. "Okay, you two. Enough. It's the next line that matters."

She picked up from where Ander had left off. "*'The album had a powerful influence on me as I prepared for my own performance of the piece at the Kentwood Philharmonic.'*"

A ripple of excitement flowed through Stella. She grinned and laid a hand gently on Mac's back. "Dammit, Mac. You hit the bullseye."

Mac raised a finger. "Not yet. I still have one more *coup de grâce*. See? The date of the review was six months ago. I cross-checked the date of the review with the schedule of the Kentwood Philharmonic."

She clicked another tab to bring up the philharmonic's website. "The only performer to have played that Grieg thing is this lady."

Stella recognized Alice20 immediately. Her dark eyes gazed out of the screen. One side of her head was shaved, while her black hair hung low over the other. Here, too, as that morning, she wore a black tank top. Her fierce, focused eyes and cherry red lipstick, likely the only color she wore, promised passion beneath her stern appearance.

Ander broke the silence. "Lisa Kerne. She's our Alice20?"

Mac shrugged. "I just bring you the results. What they mean is up to you. She looks kinda serious, though, doesn't she?"

Stella nodded and reached for her keys. "Yeah. Might be just a stupid comment on a website, but it's still worth following up. Maybe she can help us find Boris too. Thanks, Mac. Great work. Now get some rest. We'll see you tomorrow."

Since Mac was yawning, she waved.

Stella stopped in the doorway. "Coming, Ander? We've got a date at the philharmonic."

## 21

Hagen lifted his foot from the gas and let the Explorer drift down Kentwood's main street. It was empty.

The home furnishing boutique had gone out of business. No one sat at the table outside the ice cream parlor. A soft gleam of light illuminated a series of guitars in the music store window. The toy store window, filled with wooden toy houses, appeared haunted.

One police cruiser sat parked against the curb in the middle of the street.

Two others drove up and down, patrolling a zone that had almost no one in it.

A *whoop-whoop* sounded behind him, and Hagen pulled over.

"What the hell? I was barely moving."

Chloe snorted. "You certainly weren't blocking traffic either."

He and Chloe waited for the patrol officer to approach the window before flashing their badges.

The officer rocked on his heels. "Wait here." He stepped back and talked into the radio on his shoulder.

Hagen drummed his fingers on the steering wheel. A few minutes passed before the radio squawked a confirmation, and the officer wished them both a good evening.

"Chief Gray's certainly stepped up the security." Chloe watched the trees move by in shadow.

They passed the center of town and continued on the suburban roads where the richest residents lived.

Chloe watched a private security car drive toward them. "Looks like the residents have stepped up security too."

Hagen nodded. "Yeah. People like this are used to having things easy. They lock their doors at night and set the alarms, and they sleep easy, knowing nothing can ever hurt them. Then something *does* hurt them, and they don't know what to do. Everything they thought would keep them safe has proven to be wrong."

"So they reach for more of what they know best? Even more private security?"

Hagen turned off the road and started up the hill toward Jeremy Deem's house. "Might work too."

Chloe frowned. "Private security won't catch the killer. They won't even try."

"No. But they might put him off. A professional killer will find their way around these guys. But if our killer isn't a pro, and I don't think he is, the sight of all this security could deter him."

Chloe kicked back in her seat, stretching out her legs as far as she could. "Not what *we* need, though. Spook the guy, and we'll never find him. He could go to ground. Then, when everything cools down, he'll pop right back up again. They're putting off the inevitable."

Hagen agreed with Chloe. This killer wasn't going to stop. The murders felt like a vendetta, payback. He could relate. Someone with a grudge would wait for the security firms to leave and then strike.

They had to find him. These guards weren't making the search any easier.

Hagen reached the gate to the Deems' property. An officer held up a hand as they approached. Hagen rolled down his window, and they showed him their badges.

The officer waved them through, one shoulder resting wearily against the gate's pillar. "The investigators have gone for the day but don't park in front of the house. They haven't finished hunting for tire tracks yet. When you reach the bottom of the drive, you'll see a black BMW. Park behind it."

Hagen kept his foot on the brake. "Whose BMW?"

"The son's. He rolled up about an hour ago."

Chloe peered up at the officer through Hagen's window. "And you let him in? Christ, Officer. This is a crime scene."

The officer sighed deeply. "Tell me about it. The guy screamed bloody murder when I wouldn't let him in. He called Chief Gray. She told me he could come in as long as he didn't go anywhere near the crime scene. What was I supposed to do?"

"Go with him, Officer. Jeez." Chloe flopped back against her seat. "Let's go."

Hagen headed down the driveway and parked behind Jem Deem's black BMW.

The front door of the house was ajar. Pushing the door open with his fingertips and with one hand on the grip of his gun, Hagen called inside.

"Mr. Deem?"

There was no reply. The house was unnaturally quiet. Hagen stepped inside.

Without the bodies, the living room looked almost normal. Yellow triangles still indicated bullet holes. A nail on the wall showed where the Rhodell painting had once hung. The piano still stood in the corner, its lid open, the black and white keys ready to be played.

Upstairs, a door creaked open. Hagen and Chloe exchanged glances.

Chloe pointed at herself and indicated she would lead. He nodded and followed her up to the landing.

The stairs were wide enough to walk side by side, but they stayed single file.

From a room opposite the topmost landing came a quiet sob. Chloe stepped forward and touched the door.

"Mr. Deem? It's Agent Chloe Foster with the FBI. I'm coming in."

She nudged the door open.

Jem sat on the end of his parents' bed.

In his lap, he held his mother's jewelry box. His cheeks were red, and his eyes were wet. As the door swung open, he wiped his face on the sleeve of his t-shirt and closed the box.

"What are you…how did you…?"

"You left the door open downstairs."

Jem took a deep breath, gathering himself. "Did I? Sorry. This place doesn't feel like home now. I guess I should be leaving everything open so you people can all just walk in and out like it's your workplace or something."

"Actually, yeah." Though her words could be construed as callous, she was gentle.

Jem sighed. "I don't know what the hell I'm going to do with it now."

Hagen rested an arm against the doorpost. "What are you doing here, Mr. Deem?"

Jem spread his fingers over the lid of the jewelry box. "I came for my mother's things. I want my wife and daughter to have them."

This was not going to be an easy conversation. Hagen stepped past Chloe. "You'll have to wait. This place is still a crime scene, and this house and its contents need to be inventoried before you come in."

Jem stood, his face reddening as he held the jewelry box against his hip. "These were my mother's things, and I can do with them whatever the hell I want, *whenever* the hell I want. Now get out!"

Chloe took a quick step forward and placed both hands around the box. "We'll take good care of your mother's things."

He glared at her.

Chloe was clearly in no mood. "Don't even think about it. You won't like the consequences."

Jem stood for a moment, undecided.

At last, he released the box and stormed out of the room. Hagen followed him as far as the landing and watched him stride out of the front door. Then he returned to the bedroom.

Chloe slid the jewelry box back onto the dressing table. "That guy. I'm telling you, the more I talk to him, the more I think Ander might be right."

Hagen leaned against the doorjamb, arms folded across his chest. "I don't know. Maybe he's always aggressive. Or maybe it's the grief talking. Losing your entire family in one day? Does strange things to people."

"Yeah, it can make strange people even stranger." Chloe brushed past him and headed for the stairs. She stopped before she descended. "He goes crying to the chief, and we'll get it in the ear from Slade."

Hagen shrugged and followed her back downstairs to the living room. "Like you care. We came to check one thing. Let's take a look and get out of here."

The piano was impossibly big up close. It reminded Hagen of a Ferrari he'd once seen in a downtown parking lot, its sleek lines and curves out of place next to the Jeeps and Chevy pickups.

Beneath the propped-up piano lid were banks of knobs and long lines of evenly spaced wires.

Hagen kept his hands in his pockets, careful to avoid touching the piano's polished black panels.

"See anything out of place?"

Chloe walked around to the far side of the piano. She shook her head. "Doesn't look like there're any wires missing. Guess we could ask a piano expert, but I think we'd notice if there were a gap in the strings."

"Right." Hagen straightened his back. "We're definitely talking premeditation, then. The killer chose to kill this way for a reason. And they're someone with access to piano wire."

## 22

The grand foyer of the Kentwood Philharmonic was full when Stella and Ander arrived. Couples stood in polite groups. Women glittered in jewels and silky gowns. The men wore jackets and starched shirts, though most had surrendered to the evening heat and removed their ties. Everyone was posed, holding glasses of wine and laughing on cue, their teeth as shiny and gleaming as their gemstones.

Stella ran a hand over her white blouse and brushed lint off her dark slacks. "I feel underdressed."

Ander eyed her outfit. "You still look a hundred times better than anyone here. Yours truly included." His suit was rumpled after their long day. "They're all overdressed."

Stella's cheeks warmed. If they'd been in the office, she'd tell him to stuff it. But here, in the entrance to the auditorium, surrounded by carefully coiffed women, the compliment hit the right note.

"Let's find Lisa Kerne."

"She'll know where to find her." Ander indicated the far corner where the philharmonic's director stood next to the auditorium door. Amy Cooper was one of the few people in the room not holding a glass of something. She was flanked by two couples, the men gray-haired and balding, the women dripping in sparkling jewelry.

She saw them coming and excused herself. Face drawn, the smile she offered them tonight was stiff and formal compared to the sunny grin she showed the sponsors.

When she reached Stella, she flicked her head toward the side of the room, an unambiguous sign to follow her through the crowd to the offices, which they did.

As the door swung shut behind them, the burble and bustle of the conversation in the foyer faded. They were in a different world with all the construction. Bare drywall flanked the walls, and electrical wire hung in loops from the ceiling. A cable snaked across the floor, ready to trip the unwary.

Amy folded her arms. She looked like a teacher about to interrogate troublemaking students.

Maybe to the everyday person, the stance would be intimidating. Two FBI agents weren't going to be cowed, however. Stella suppressed a smile. "Where can we find Lisa Kerne?"

Amy blinked as if she hadn't heard the question correctly. "You...you can't. I mean, not *now*. The performance is about to begin. It's a special benefit for local food banks, a performance Jeremy Deem himself insisted on each year. And why on earth would you want to speak to Lisa?"

Ander stepped forward. The top of his head brushed the bottom of a loop of wire. "Where can we find her?"

Amy's nostrils flared. "Look. Please. You have to understand. Lisa is...she's a remarkable talent, but she's...she can be very temperamental. I don't know if she'd be able to play after..." The level of panic the director displayed was interesting to witness. "I only ask you to speak to her *after* the performance. I have an almost-full auditorium, and...this is a special occasion. I'm sure the FBI wouldn't want to ruin a performance for such a good cause?"

Ander looked about as annoyed as Stella felt. "I don't—"

"Listen." She touched Stella's arm and offered her sunny sponsor smile. "One of our supporters had to cancel, so I have an empty box tonight. Why don't you wait there? Watch the performance, and when the show is over, you can speak to her as much as you want."

The director clearly thought Stella was the weak link. She hadn't come here to attend a music performance. Stella didn't need Amy Cooper's permission to speak to Lisa Kerne or anyone.

"Or we could just—"

"That might not be a bad idea," Ander said.

Stella arched an eyebrow at Ander, not hiding her irritation.

He rushed to explain before Stella's gaze set him on fire. "She's not going anywhere. Could be useful to see her in action. And she'll probably be more relaxed after her performance." Ander offered his own sunny smile. "And a concert might be nice."

Amy's hands came together in a prayer, pleading silently with Stella, begging her not to disturb the evening's performance.

Stella sighed. "Fine. We'll talk to her after the show."

Amy breathed out in relief. "Thank you. And I know you'll love the concert. It really is something special."

Before the director could move away, Stella caught her arm. "Do you know anything about a musician known as Boris the Boringest online?"

Amy sniffed. "Yes, of course. Why?"

Stella ignored the question. "Do you know who attended that particular performance?"

Lines marred the director's forehead. "No. Should I?"

Disappointment punched Stella in the gut. They were still waiting to hear from the Budapest Philharmonic regarding the event, but their administrative assistant was on vacation. Stella hoped Amy could provide the information sooner. "I was hoping you might have coordinated the event that led up to that performance. Or maybe knew who did?"

Amy tapped her bottom lip. "I would assume Mr. Deem's assistant? Karen Neuglass?"

"Not according to Ms. Neuglass."

"Well, it certainly wasn't me." Amy glanced at her watch. "Let's get you to your seats."

She led them back into the foyer and spoke to one of the ushers, a tall young man in black pants and a purple vest. He led them up a narrow set of stairs into a small box overlooking the stage. Four seats, all larger than the chairs in the lower levels, sat empty.

Was this where the Deems had been meant to sit?

Onstage, the orchestra warmed up, sending violin scrapes and trumpet blasts into the hall. The usher handed Ander a program before wishing them a good evening.

Ander eased into one of the chairs and stretched his legs. "Here you go." He handed her the program. "This is the life. About time this job gave us some perks."

Stella settled into the seat next to him, dropping the program on the floor.

He wasn't wrong. Sitting in a private box with a grandstand view was a rare treat. And she hadn't enjoyed any treats in a very long time.

*Ring.*

Stella yanked her phone out of her pocket. The sight of Chloe's name on the screen added a short burst of guilt. Chloe and Hagen were off doing real investigative work while she and Ander relaxed a little.

"We're leaving Jeremy Deem's house right now."

Stella closed her eyes and shut out the auditorium. "Find anything?"

"Not really. The M.E. thinks one of the murder weapons was piano wire, but there's no wire missing from the Deems' piano. If he's right, the killer brought it with him. We're talking about a premeditated murder committed by someone I'm betting has connections to the music world."

"Right." Stella opened her eyes, feeling like—surprisingly—she and Ander might be at the right place at the right time. She peered over the edge of the box and down at the stage. Only the pianist's chair was empty now, the lid of the grand piano propped open.

Chloe's voice wavered in and out. Stella could tell she and Hagen were in a moving vehicle. "Anyway, we'll hope for a quiet night and pick it up again tomorrow. Hey, listen. I'm going to the hospital to see Dani after Hagen drops me at my car. Want to meet me there?"

Stella hesitated. Visiting Dani did sound attractive. It was a normal thing normal people did, and she could benefit from something normal in her life.

Ander nudged her. "Is that Chloe?"

"Yeah. She's on her way to visit Dani."

"Cool. Tell her to wish Dani the best for me. And if Dani's looking for baby names, tell her Ander's a great one."

"They had a girl."

Ander lifted a shoulder. "Could still work."

Stella laughed and refocused on the call. "We're waiting to speak to Lisa Kerne. Could take a while. We have to sit through the concert first. Say hi to Dani for me, though, and give the baby a big kiss."

Applause echoed through the auditorium. Stella wrapped the call up and set the phone to vibrate.

Amy Cooper walked onto the stage with regal grace.

When she reached the front, she took the microphone in one hand. The applause died away.

"Thank you, and welcome to our sixth annual benefit for our neighboring food banks. Last year, the generosity of our patrons enabled us to buy enough food to supply more than five hundred low-income families with one meal daily for a year."

Applause rang through the auditorium again. Someone whistled.

*The rich like to applaud themselves, I guess.*

Amy raised a hand. The noise fell. "And none of it would have been possible without the support, the generosity, and the encouragement of our late board member, Jeremy Deem."

She paused. A thick and heavy silence filled the room.

"Jeremy's tragic death has struck us all. He, his wife, and her mother were much-loved members of our community and dedicated supporters of the arts."

The director lowered the microphone, but not before it sent the sound of a sniffle echoing through the hall. She took a deep breath and straightened her back.

"Tonight's benefit is dedicated to Jeremy and his beloved family. And now, let me introduce our pianist, Lisa Kerne."

Amy turned and extended an arm as Lisa Kerne strode onto the stage. The performer wore a long black dress topped with a square of white lace stretching to her throat. A black ribbon circled her neck. Her long hair had been pushed to one side, revealing the shaved scalp above her temple and rows of silver earrings. A delicate chain ran over the top of her ear and swung against her neck, glinting in the stage lights.

Stella leaned toward Ander. "Guess Donovan Freeman didn't give enough to be acknowledged."

"Skinflint." Ander shook his head. "But the news might not have spread yet."

Lisa sat on her stool and stretched her arms, her fingers clasped, while Amy tiptoed off the stage.

The house lights fell. The orchestra dropped into darkness until only a single spotlight remained on the pianist, her head bowed in front of the piano.

In the shadows, the conductor raised his baton. He held it for a moment, then brought his arm down in a sweeping arc.

The violins started first, the cellos joining in a moment later, deepening the sound and filling the hall with a brief, mournful tone.

Stella picked up her program. Ferruccio Busoni's Piano Concerto in D Minor, op. 17.

She'd never heard of Busoni, and she'd never heard this piece either.

As Lisa Kerne added the piano, her hands bouncing up and down on the keys as though her fingers were children jumping on a trampoline, the auditorium's collective mood shifted to happiness and anticipation.

Something was growing, about to burst into life. Those joyful, clipped, rapid keystrokes were all-consuming, making it impossible to believe anything bad could ever happen.

Lisa played on, the piano riding over the strings and carrying the audience higher and higher. Stella glanced at her colleague.

Ander's eyes were fixed on the stage, his head and shoulders swaying in time with the music, as though he were alone in the box, alone in the auditorium.

As he moved with the pianist, Stella smiled. Ander was a strong, handsome man with a simple, straightforward appeal.

Hagen was smooth until you hit a sharp edge that was hiding in the shadows. She didn't know how to maneuver through that part of his personality.

In Ander, there was no pretense. She always knew what he was thinking and what he was feeling. Time with him was easy and strangely refreshing.

Between the music and the company, Stella found thoughts of piano wire garroting fading away.

Ander caught her eye. "She's very good. Might add this song to my playlist."

"Right after Joan Jett."

He grinned and gave her a thumbs-up.

Stella smiled and settled back in her seat.

The concert continued, with Lisa Kerne playing pieces from Grieg and Rachmaninoff and ending with Beethoven. Her performance brought the audience to its feet with cries of "encore" and "bravo." Stella found herself standing alongside Ander, applauding as hard as the rest of them.

Lisa played one more piece, then exited the stage after the briefest of bows.

Stella touched Ander's arm. "That's our cue."

He stopped applauding and followed her out of the box. They descended to a lobby that was already filling with audience members checking their phones and digging into their pockets for car keys.

A sign above a door toward the back of the lobby said *Stage Entrance*. Without waiting, Stella pushed it open and stepped into a narrow corridor made narrower by sheets of plywood and coils of cable. The walls were marred with scuff marks from a series of leaning ladders.

They continued around the back of the stage until they reached a door that opened as they drew near.

A short man in a dark suit came out. He held a cello case big enough to hide most of his face. As Stella and Ander approached, he lowered the case and frowned at them.

Ander pointed at the room. "Lisa Kerne?"

The cellist's face fell even further. "Yeah, *she's* in there."

Stella and Ander exchanged a look before Stella opened the door and entered the room.

Another musician in a dark suit was carefully strapping a violin into a case. Two other players perched on the edge of a dressing table, sipping soft drinks from cans. A trombonist stretched his instrument until it separated in two.

Against the far wall, Lisa Kerne sat at a dressing table covered with bouquets. Some vases contained the typical dozen roses. Others were filled with the contents of a botanical garden.

She removed an earring and placed it in a box nestled between the plush legs of a toy rabbit.

Stella squeezed between the musicians, ignoring their confused glances until she reached the end of the room.

She pulled out her ID. "Lisa Kerne? I'm Special Agent Stella Knox with the FBI, and this is my colleague, Ander Bennett."

Lisa turned, both hands still at her left ear. She squinted at Stella's ID as though she were reading each word carefully, trying out their sounds in her head. Changing the tempo, adjusting the key.

Behind Stella, the room fell silent, and she could almost feel everyone listening.

The pianist, done with Stella's ID, dropped the earring into the box. "If you want an autograph, I'm afraid I don't do them. Or selfies."

Her voice was deeper than Stella expected, but Lisa drew out her vowels like most Tennesseans.

Stella put away her ID. "Lisa, the YouTube profile Alice20. Is it yours?"

At the end of the room, someone whispered, "Five minutes, then boom."

"Ten bucks says three," came an equally quiet reply.

"Done."

Lisa lifted her head. "Is *what* mine?"

"Alice20." Stella pulled her phone from her pocket and showed Lisa the video of *Boris the Boringest* and her comment beneath it.

Lisa's face froze, but she recovered quickly and waved the screen away. "Oh, that. We're talking what? Two…three years ago? I should have been more…I don't know…diplomatic, I suppose. But they were very rude, putting a video like that on the internet. Things live forever on the World Wide Web. It's so inconsiderate. So…humiliating. It made me furious. Think of the poor musician. No one ever does."

"Do you know the musician?"

"Of course." Lisa lifted her chin.

Stella gritted her teeth. "What's his name?"

"Boris."

*Dear God, please save me from throttling this woman.*

"Boris what?"

"Just Boris. He's mononymous." Lisa lifted an eyebrow. "Do you need a definition?"

Stella ignored the jab. "He may only go by one name onstage, perhaps, but what about his legal name? The one from his birth certificate?"

Lisa pulled out a drawer. "I'm not his mother, and thus, am not privy to such a document."

This was getting them nowhere.

Stella raised her phone. "Do you recognize any of the people in the audience?"

Lisa pulled a cloth from a packet of makeup remover and wiped her cheek. She gave the phone screen a brief glance. "No, why? Should I?"

Stella moved the screen closer to Lisa's face. "Look again."

Lisa rolled her eyes. She watched for a moment, then pushed a bouquet of gardenias aside to clear a space in front of the mirror before reaching for a pot of moisturizer. "Still no."

Ander pointed toward the screen. "The guy with his mouth open is Jeremy Deem. Remember him? Your director mentioned him tonight. He's been murdered. The guy two rows behind him? Donovan Freeman. He's also a subscriber to this philharmonic. Also murdered."

Lisa paused her skin care routine. "I don't know who this Donovan guy is. I've met Jeremy Deem. Now you mention it, I guess that does look like him. Hard to tell with all those shadows."

Stella scrolled to the comments. "This comment beneath this video? That's you hoping they both burn in hell."

Lisa dabbed cream beneath her eyes. Her voice was calm when she spoke, seeming unaffected by the news of the two murders. "I guess I got my wish, then. I expect burning is exactly what they're both doing now."

The ice in Lisa's voice gave Stella goose bumps.

Lisa tossed her dirty wipe into the trash and put the lid back on her moisturizer. She turned to face Ander, paler than a few moments before. "But if you think I had something to do with their deaths, Agent, then you're way off. I didn't even remember who these people were until thirty seconds ago when you reminded me. I was just angry." She shrugged her narrow shoulders. "People should show more respect."

Stella put her phone away, but she wasn't quite ready to lighten up on Lisa. "Where were you on Saturday night?"

Lisa pushed her chair back and stood. "That's easy. I was right here from about three p.m. until after midnight. Or rather, I was either in my dressing room or onstage. Witnessed by five hundred and twenty-three people. Is that enough? Do you need to count the orchestra members as well?"

Stella ignored the sarcasm. "And Sunday?"

Her lips turned up at the corners, but the gesture only vaguely resembled a smile. "Same thing. Different five hundred people." The musician took a black leather handbag from the back of the chair. She dropped her jewelry box into its depths and then closed it with a loud snap. "Now, if you'll excuse me. I need to rest. I have another performance tomorrow."

She gathered her bouquets, cradling them carefully in one arm, and pushed her chair back to give herself more space to leave.

Ander lifted the toy rabbit from the dressing table. "Don't forget your friend."

Lisa snatched the stuffed animal from Ander's hand. She moved so fast she dropped her flowers. The bouquets tumbled to the ground. Her voice rose until it was almost a scream. "How dare you? Don't you *dare* touch him."

The other musicians in the changing area stopped talking. The players with the coke cans froze mid-drink, and the trombonist held his brass above his instrument box.

"That was three." One of the coke drinkers turned and slipped a ten to the trombonist.

Lisa ignored them. She pushed the toy back into place, straightening the animal's long ears so they were in exactly the same position as before.

Ander lifted his hands in mock surrender. "Sorry. Didn't mean to offend. My son had a toy like that. We forgot it once in a restaurant during a road trip. Nonstop tears. I had to drive back two hours to find it." He paused. "His was a dog, though. Not a rabbit."

Lisa folded the toy's left ear. She spoke quietly, her voice little louder than a hiss. "I don't give a damn about rabbits. He just reminds me of *Alice in Wonderland*. And now, I'm going to ask both of you to leave."

Stella glanced at Ander, who shrugged. They had what they needed—Lisa's airtight alibi for both murders. They could question her about what time she left and what she did afterward, but it didn't matter. At the exact time the rabbit had knocked on the victims' doors, Lisa Kerne had been sitting in front of hundreds of people.

They made their way back to the foyer. The entrance was almost empty now.

Two pairs of couples stood in opposite corners, standing close and talking quietly. They were still clutching their wine glasses and didn't appear to be in any hurry to end their evening.

Ander held the door open for Stella. "Want to get a drink before we call it a night? It's been a long day, and I gotta tell you, I could do with something to wash that interview out of my head."

The night had been a roller-coaster. Three hours ago, she'd been at a crime scene. Ten minutes ago, she'd been sitting in a box at the philharmonic, enjoying some beautiful classical music with a good-looking man who made her laugh. A minute ago, she'd been talking to a potential suspect about a murder.

"Yeah. Let's go."

Before they could head out, a hand landed on Ander's shoulder.

The trombonist stood right behind him, his expression serious. "Always rabbits with Lisa. Never touch the bunny."

## 23

Sis sat at Coco's, the café under Stella's apartment, and slid the menu across the table. A couple strolled under the lights on the other side of the street. They seemed so happy, so trusting. He led her by the arm, and she, the idiot, let him.

She picked up the saltshaker. It was glass, heavy with a rounded, metal top.

If she threw it hard enough, she could pitch it over the cars and slam it into the back of the man's head. As he rubbed his crown, he'd release his girlfriend, and she'd be free. She could make a run for it and wouldn't have to live like every other woman—forced to do whatever a damn man wanted.

Sis could do whatever she wanted. She was free. Freedom was more important than anything.

Stella wasn't free. She was the type who always did the right thing, trapped by duty. Miss Goody Two-Shoes, always ready to sacrifice herself for others.

*Ugh. What a waste of time.*

What Stella didn't know—what people like her could

never understand—was everyone was out to screw everyone else. Even the people who swore they loved you. They were all in it for themselves, and the only way to avoid being their victim was to make sure you screwed them first. That's how the world worked.

"Here you go, darlin'." The server slid a large plate of a burger and fries onto the table. "Anything else I can get you?"

Sis lifted the bun. "Yeah, bring me some hot sauce. Not the cheap, mild stuff you give the tourists. I want the extra hot stuff. The kind that'll blow the roof of your mouth off."

The server grinned. "I think we got some in back." She lowered her voice. "We keep it in a special secure container."

As the woman headed back to the kitchen, Sis squeezed some ketchup onto her plate and dipped a fry.

It was a shame Stella wasn't in the café now. She'd like to have been able to sit here and watch her, listen in on her phone calls, and check out what she was eating for supper. But being this close to her apartment, in this café Stella visited regularly, was almost like slipping into Stella's life. Sis could see without being seen, exactly the way she liked it.

Only her brother was dumb enough to keep following someone around like a lost puppy. There were other ways to find out what she needed to know.

Chewing a fry, Sis pushed an earbud into her ear and picked up her phone.

She played the recording from the night before. Stella's voice sounded in Sis's head, dulled and tinned by the bug's small microphone, but it was definitely hers.

She must have been on the phone, yammering on about babies and something about therapy.

*"You know what would help me? Finding my father's killer and bringing him to justice. An army of therapists couldn't have as much impact."*

So Stella wasn't just looking for a reunion with her old

uncle. She really wanted to find out who killed her daddy. Would she try to bring all the powers of the FBI with her?

*Idiot girl.*

Sis stopped the playback and pulled out the earbud. *That was information The Officer would be very interested to hear.*

But there was still too much she didn't know.

Stella's friend, for example.

Hagen.

Was that who she'd been talking to?

She thought back to their encounter in the park with his big, slobbering dog that wouldn't have been able to catch a frisbee if Hagen had duct-taped it to his mouth.

Bubs.

Stupid name for such a big animal.

Hagen was an attractive man, no doubt. Sharp and confident. But there was also a fire behind those dark green eyes of his, something burning back there. She'd recognized those flames right away, though he did well to hide them.

What was his agenda here? Surely he wasn't lending a hand and putting himself at risk out of the goodness of his heart.

*Naw, he had to have his own reason.*

Could be something as simple as an old-fashioned crush. Maybe Stella and her dark eyes had crumbled Hagen's granite façade. But perhaps there was more to it.

A little pillow talk might loosen those soft lips of his.

"When a duty becomes a pleasure." She popped another fry into her mouth.

Poor fool. He had no idea what he'd gotten himself mixed up in.

The server returned, a small bottle of chili sauce in her hand. She set it on the table. "You sure you want this stuff, hun? Practically scorch off your taste buds. I think the chef uses it to clean the stove."

Sis poured a drop from the bottle onto her fingertip. She lifted her finger to her lips, felt the tingle, sucked it off. At first, the heat warmed the surface of her tongue, but soon, a blaze spread to the back of her throat like wildfire.

"That's the stuff." She lifted her bun and shook the sauce over the burger until it covered every inch of meat. "You keep this stuff for the regulars, huh?"

The server took back the bottle, holding it gingerly between her finger and thumb as if the glass itself would burn. "The ones who know to ask for it. Not many people do."

Sis licked another dollop of sauce off her finger, embracing the heat. "Bet the people who live here are keen. Got sauce like this under your nose, you're not going to miss out."

The server grinned. "Oh, I don't know. We got our regulars, but I don't think any of them go for this stuff. Some of them still got taste buds."

Sis picked up the burger. "Is that right? What do the regulars go for? I should know for next time I come by."

"Oh, you know, the usual. The eggs benedict goes down a treat in the mornings, and the waffles are always popular."

"Uh-huh. That's the regular breakfast, is it?"

"For most people. There's one woman who always has hot cocoa in the morning, and she's got a real hankering for chocolate chip cookies." The waitress leaned closer and lowered her voice. "I think she's in the CIA or something."

Sis did her best to appear impressed. "Wow. Real celebrities you get in here. She only come in for breakfast?"

"Naw, she sometimes meets a friend here in the evening. They like to sit out near the street. Probably so she can watch for Russian spies or something."

Sis made a mental note—*table by the street*. Another table sat right behind it. Sitting there, she should be able to hear everything Stella said.

Heck, she might even be able to stick a little bug onto the underside of Stella's preferred table.

The waitress returned to the kitchen, holding the chili bottle at arm's length.

Sis bit into her burger. Apart from the fire burning somewhere beneath the bun, she couldn't taste too much. The numbness in her mouth when she finished was refreshing. She enjoyed every second of her scorching hot burger.

Leaving the café, she crossed the road and glanced up at Stella's window. Miss Special Agent still wasn't back.

Either Stella was working late, or she was out having a good time.

Perhaps with Hagen.

And while killers were on the loose.

*"Tsk-tsk."*

*Don't you care about all these innocent people?*

She laughed to herself and called The Officer. The phone rang twice.

"What you got?"

The Officer's lack of pleasantries didn't bother Sis. He'd always been direct. He always would be. And he was right. Why beat about the bush?

"Our friend isn't just looking to chat with our Joel. She wants to find the guy behind her dad's killing. Straight from the horse's mouth."

The phone went silent for a moment. "Good. Now we know what she wants."

"Yeah, and I know what *I* want. We're wasting time now. Let me—"

"Enough." The sound of his breath was heavy through the phone. "If we have to, we will. *You* will. But only if we must. I want to know how close she is first. And if she's talking to one person about her daddy's death, she's probably talking to more. We need a list. Get back in there and see what else you can find."

The line went dead.

Disappointed, Sis slipped the phone back into her pocket and turned into a dark alley.

*He's taking too long, the old man. He's too hesitant. If he doesn't decide soon, we're all lost.*

## 24

Stella laughed so hard her sides were sore. Her jaw ached. A couple sitting on the other side of the Badger Bar's U-shaped counter stared at her with a mixture of concern and envy.

She didn't care. For the first time in a long time, she was laughing without restraint and without guilt. She was on her second dirty martini.

Although Ander was nursing his Negroni so he could drive her home afterward, his impression of their colleague, Martin Lin, had been so spot-on, she couldn't help but burst out laughing.

Martin Lin was a native New Yorker. Even though he'd transferred to Nashville almost three years ago, Martin still talked and walked as though he were a cop in Queens. He was devoted to adventure sports, and the only thing more exciting to him than jumping off a cliff was telling everyone about it afterward.

"So there I was, sliding down the side of Everest on a surfboard." Ander elongated his vowels and added a nasal tone—an accent that should've drowned somewhere in the East River. "When I meet the Yeti coming the other way. Well, he hops onto my board, and we ride down to base camp together."

Stella sipped her martini. "Do you think *any* of his stories are true?"

Ander shrugged, popping a few peanuts in his mouth. "I dunno. He does the kind of stuff sane people wouldn't go anywhere near. Did you hear about the time he gave demolition derby a go?"

"No!" Stella tried to imagine Martin Lin behind the wheel of a smashed-up sedan, his gelled hair grazing the dented ceiling. It was like trying to picture a fish flying a plane.

"Caleb put him up to it. Told him it was something no city boy could do. Caleb isn't a city boy, but it did the trick. So Martin signs up, and we all went along to watch."

"Let me guess. His ride got squashed into pulp."

Ander shook his head. "Nope. We thought he'd treat the whole thing like a race, you know? Try to zoom around the track and smash nose-first into the wall at the first bend. He didn't. He drove like an old lady steering a go-kart. Putted around at the back, steered clear of everyone else. Whenever a car came near, he'd *stop*. When the derby ended, the car was in better condition than when he started. Hagen spent days trying to explain to him how the thing should have worked. Martin wasn't having any of it."

Stella laughed until she hiccupped. "And Hagen went to this? Wasn't he worried about getting his precious shoes dirty?"

Ander rolled the bottom of his glass over the counter. "Yeah. Not his usual thing either. At one point, he talked about putting plastic bags over his shoes to keep the mud off."

Stella slapped her hand to her mouth. She could see Hagen standing in the crowd in his pressed jeans and polo shirt, two mud-spattered plastic bags protecting his Italian Oxfords.

"Yeah, he's a good guy, Hagen. You like him, right?" Ander took a sip of his cocktail. His effort to stay casual was clear as day.

Stella's face warmed. She sipped her drink again, hoping the glass was big enough to hide the color in her cheeks. She wasn't sure what to say. She wasn't even sure what to tell herself.

"Yeah, he's a good guy. Kinda...closed. But yeah, he's nice."

"And are you two—"

Stella lowered her glass.

*That was direct. What the hell were people in the office thinking?*

"We're just friends."

Ander gave a small nod and leaned back. He seemed unconvinced. "Friends who spent a weekend together." He held up a hand to cut off whatever she was going to say...if she'd known what to say. "It's none of my business. I get it. Really. It's just...Hagen's a good friend, and he's been pretty quiet since you arrived. I don't know what's going on, but I... hey, I don't want to get in the way."

She hesitated. Ander might think she and Hagen were crazy in their pursuit of answers. She didn't know if she should include one more person. Once again, she was back on difficult ground, making difficult decisions, forced to think again about her father's death.

Maybe Mac was right. They'd only made small steps so far. Important steps. Small but safe ones. From here, the going would get tougher. The further she advanced in her investigation, the closer she got to the person who'd ordered her father's death, the harder and more dangerous her search would become.

At the moment, she had Mac on her side, doing research and hitting up her inside sources for information.

And she had Hagen on the ground.

*Or did she?*

He'd been okay so far, but when push came to shove, Stella wasn't completely sure he'd be there. It was a horrible thought, and she knew she had little reason to believe it. But the doubt lingered. They might only be traveling in the same direction for the moment.

They weren't headed to the same destination.

And she'd need help to get where she wanted to go. She'd need support in the end.

She finished her drink, letting the vermouth flare at the back of her throat, and lowered her glass back to the bar.

"Hagen's been helping me."

Ander's blue eyes were gentle, his face welcoming, free of judgment. She could tell him. She knew she could. Ander would never do anything to hurt her, would always back her up.

She swallowed against the lump in her throat. The vermouth hadn't burned bright enough. "You know my father was a cop, right?"

Ander nodded. "That's what I heard."

"And you know he was killed in the line of duty."

He nodded again. "I'm sorry."

"Dad had a partner. A guy called Joel Ramirez. 'Uncle Joel,' I used to call him. One night, after my dad died, he came to the house, very drunk, and told me the people responsible for my father's death were dirty cops."

"Jeez, Stella. Did they ever find out who they were?"

Stella shook her head. "No. And, more importantly, we never found out who was running those cops. Unc..." She snapped her mouth shut before the rest of "uncle" could come out. "Joel was killed the next day." She went to take another drink and realized she'd already swallowed the last of her martini. "Or so I thought."

Ander's glass was halfway to his lips. He stopped. "What do you mean?"

"Mac did some digging. She found out Joel was an undercover cop who was called into Memphis PD to check out some dirty cops. Anyway, Mac found Joel's family in Atlanta."

The rim had reached Ander's lips while Stella spoke. He lowered the glass again, still without drinking. "Seriously? How'd she manage to do that?"

Stella shrugged, unwilling to give her friend away. "Says she's got sources. Don't ask me. Anyway—"

"That was why you and Hagen went to Atlanta? To speak to his family?"

Stella nodded. "Yeah. Hagen heard Mac and me talking and offered his help."

She paused, wondering if she should tell Ander about Hagen's father's death.

*No. His business is his business.*

"I appreciated the company."

"Right." Ander finally took a swig of his cocktail. It was a long one. "So what did Joel's family tell you?"

"Nothing. Didn't quite work out the way we'd planned."

Stella dragged the last olive off the cocktail stick with her teeth and popped it into her mouth. Salt burst over her tongue. "When we got to Atlanta, we found Unc…" She cleared her throat. "We found Joel. Alive. He was coming out of the house."

Ander let out a low whistle. He slid his thumb up and down the glass. "So Joel's death was…"

"Faked. And according to Mac, he's in witness protection."

Ander exhaled. He thought for a moment before he spoke. "Nice. As if your little sideline investigation wasn't tough enough. Did you speak to him?"

"No. We were about to, but Slade called us back for the cheerleaders. Haven't had a chance to get back. It's been one case after another."

"True."

She fixed her gaze on him again. Everything about his demeanor said he was open and listening. "It kinda gets worse. Just driving out there seems to have stirred up a hornet's nest. While we were up in Stonevale, I was pretty sure someone was following me. I don't think it was someone on our side. Too unprofessional. Someone wants to know what I'm up to."

Ander rested his chin on the back of his fist. He seemed to lose himself in thought for a moment. She couldn't read his expression.

Eventually, he lowered his arm, picked up his glass, and emptied it.

He returned the glass to the counter and took a deep breath.

"Stella, it sounds like you, Hagen, and Mac are playing with fire while juggling chainsaws. You're messing around with criminal gangs, with witness protection, with people who've shown they've no problem murdering law enforcement officers. I don't know what the hell Mac's playing at, getting you this information, and I don't know what the hell Hagen's doing helping you."

"I—"

"But...as long as you're doing this, you're not leaving me out. And you should tell Slade too. If anyone knows how to work this mess, it's him."

To her surprise, tears of relief rushed to Stella's eyes. She blinked hard to get rid of them. She'd shared the load, and she had friends to take the weight.

Ander dipped into his pocket and left a bill on the counter for the bartender. "Now, let's call this night a night. Our jobs just got more serious."

## 25

My 1986 Nissan Maxima made a strange grinding noise. Every few minutes, it sent out a little crunch like a bleating French horn. The noise was out of place. Discordant.

Especially in the Kentwood streets. Not only was the clunker musically out of place, but it was a physical eyesore against Porsches and BMWs. I'd be pulled over for sure.

The town was dead. It was a little past nine thirty. The stores were dark, the restaurants closed. The tables on the sidewalk were covered with upturned chairs. Sidewalks, where couples should've strolled happily, were populated by pairs of deputies and lone security guards.

All those uniforms made my stomach clench.

The environment had changed.

The first two names on my list had gone without a hitch. It had all been so easy—much easier than I'd expected.

Even using the piano wire. I thought I'd recoil at getting so close, but once I'd wrapped the metal around Jeremy Deem's neck, I was overcome with a wave of anger and rage.

I'd pulled tighter and tighter, and when the blood spurted out and sprayed over the floor...

Like the peak of a crescendo.

For three long years, I'd waited in my little beach house. I'd rarely left. I hadn't dared to. The embarrassment was too great.

Some might call it brooding.

But they'd be wrong. I wasn't brooding. I was bruised. Battered. I didn't dare show my face. Everywhere I went, I heard people laughing, saw them figuratively pointing. They all knew. They'd all seen what'd happened. What lived on the internet lived forever. A terrible immortality.

I wanted to dig myself a deep hole and lie in it until the end of the world.

The damn Nissan jerked again. The gas tank was half full, so fuel wasn't the problem. The vehicle was. It was over thirty years old. Didn't matter. Once I'd finished my list, the car wouldn't have to last much longer.

With these Philistines gone, I could return to my music and all the accolades that came with it.

I was making the world better. Not just for me. For her too.

She'd have a safer position in a world better able to appreciate her talents.

So yes, I'd deal with them. Not much longer now. The list was shorter.

The thought thrilled me.

I turned off the road, heading up the hill toward the Kentwood Estates.

A police cruiser drove toward me, the blue and red lights on the roof flashing a warning. I slowed.

As I passed a nearby home, a security guard paced in front of the gate. His flashlight highlighted the blue of his shirt. A radio was strapped next to the crest of a security firm on his shoulder, and a gun sat in the holster on his hip.

He stopped as I approached. The beam of his flashlight rose, glaring through my windshield.

I drove on, my heart thumping.

On the passenger floorboard, my gun and piano wire lay next to the rabbit mask. Even a rudimentary search of my car would find them in an instant.

I took the next turn. Another security guard sat outside the nearest house. This guard poured a drink from a thermos for a police officer whose cruiser was parked at the curb.

The guard watched me drive past. He lifted a hand in greeting, and I responded in kind, unsure whether ignoring him would be more memorable than the simple acknowledgment.

This area was too dangerous. There were too many guards, too much security.

Instead of spending their fortunes on music and musicians, the good folks of Kentwood were spending their cash on their own protection.

Very wise.

And very irritating.

Taking the road back down the hill, I headed away.

I couldn't go to the motel. My blood was up, and my heart raced. Everything I needed was right here with me. My headlights illuminated a sign marking the road to Marrowbone Lake.

I pulled into the lake's empty parking lot, the car facing the water.

My throat was dry. My fingers trembled on top of the steering wheel. I felt as if I were about to give a performance. The nerves were similar. It was like I had the first notes already in my head and the audience blocked out.

But instead of heading to the piano stool, I had to wait in the shadows. The anticipation was killing me.

*I had to act. I had to act now!*

I exhaled slowly.

*Calm yourself. There's time. There're still plenty of names on the list. You have all the time you need to deal with them.*

But if I made a move in Kentwood, they'd catch me in an instant.

And those Philistines would get away.

*Patience. Slow down. This is an* adagio *not a* presto.

Still, my heart raced, and my knee bounced up and down, knocking against the steering wheel.

I turned on the radio to the local classical station.

The long complaint of a violin filled the car. Vivaldi. "Summer." Classical radio stations always played Vivaldi. And Beethoven and Mozart and a little Bach for the "educated" listener.

With my eyes closed, I let the music flow. Outside, the lake lapped gently at the stones on the shore. Inside, the violins brought out the sun to warm the shepherd before the minor chords hinted at the arrival of the coming storm.

Soon the *presto* would start. Violins would release hail, washing away the heat and sending the shepherd and his flock fleeing. I took a deep breath.

Then came the advertisement...

*"Sknx-x-x-x! Sound like someone you know? If you or someone you know sounds like a leaf blower when they sleep, try the all-new Nosefit CPAP mask. You'll never have a quieter night."*

I clenched the steering wheel. Rage flowed through me again. I twisted the radio knob so hard it came off in my hand.

My cell phone rang, and like the dogs from Pavlov's experiment, my mouth watered in anticipation as Gustav Holst's "Mars, Bringer of War" belted from the small speaker.

I'd selected my greatest supporter's ringtone perfectly. The piece was written just before World War I began and reflected the true horror, brutality, and atrocity of war.

I was in the middle of my own personal war now. The song choice was fitting.

"Yes?"

I listened to the praise heaped upon me for yet another job well done, which was followed by, "You're not finished yet."

My heart pounded harder. "I know, but the forces against me are stronger now."

The quiet chuckle soothed my nerves. "But you are stronger. Do you have the list?"

I reached under the passenger seat and pulled out the folder containing the names of my enemies. "Yes."

"Listen closely."

By the time my greatest supporter ended the call, I was smiling once again.

## 26

Hagen rested his feet on his leather footrest and scratched the top of his dog's head.

Everything in his townhouse had its place.

The line of the square coaster under his beer glass was parallel to the edge of the table. The two remote controls lay next to his phone, each as straight and true as a couple of Marines in formation.

Even the Corona bottle was already rinsed and placed upright in the kitchen's recycling bin.

Only Bubs was out of place. The cushion meant to serve as his dog's bed sat in the corner of the room, unused.

Instead, Bubs stretched across the sofa, his head in Hagen's lap.

Hagen sipped his second beer from his glass.

On television, Steph Curry leapt through the air, one arm outstretched, completing a dunk for the Warriors. The move was majestic, but Hagen barely noticed.

His mind was somewhere else. Not even Curry's athleticism could bring it back.

Stella was at the philharmonic with Ander. He'd been

sitting right next to Chloe when she'd called Stella. The thought of Stella and Ander at the concert, enjoying classical music together, burned his stomach.

He scratched Bubs's head harder. "I'm being an idiot, aren't I, boy? I think you're rubbing off on me."

Bubs gave a soft *ruff*.

Stella and Ander were working the case. That was the only reason they'd gone to the philharmonic.

They needed to speak to the pianist, especially now that they knew one of the murder weapons was likely to be piano wire.

Still, the thought of Ander and Stella—together—rankled him.

Heck, he would have appreciated the music much more than Ander. Hagen's parents used to take him to classical concerts all the time. They thought a bit of symphony would be good for him and his sisters. The Yates children would grow up cultured and educated, able to discuss composers. His dad even encouraged him to learn the violin for a while, until Hagen won a spot on the basketball team.

Sports and girls easily overtook rosin and scales.

*Dammit.*

He reached for his phone. The line rang and rang.

*Too long. He shouldn't take this long to answer. I guess he must be—*

"Hey, Hagen. Whatcha up to?"

Hagen scratched Bubs's ear harder. Bubs put up a paw, pushing Hagen's hand down.

Ander was way too perky. Hagen tried to keep his own tone light and casual. "Wanted to know how the chat with the pianist went. You still there with Stella?"

"Just dropped her off. Got a free concert, man. Who says this job doesn't have any perks?"

"Not me. That vending machine at the resident agency? That's why I joined the Bureau."

"Ha, knew I'd get you into those health bars eventually. Yeah, we spoke to the pianist after the concert. She's a strange fish. And a cold one. Got a connection to the victims and access to pianos. Definitely aggressive. But her alibi is rock solid. I dunno. Feels like a big stretch. We'd need to find a better motive than irritation at a three-year-old YouTube video."

"Right. Probably worth keeping an eye on her, though." Hagen paused. "How *was* the concert?"

"Sounded good to me, but what do I know? Stella seemed to have a good time."

Hagen patted Bubs's head a little too hard. The dog rolled over, teetering on the edge of the couch.

Ander seemed not to notice any tension. "It was good to see her enjoying herself. We went for a drink afterward. I think it was the first time I've seen her laugh."

Hagen buried his fingers deep in Bubs's fur, partly to steady himself and partly to keep Bubs from falling off the couch. His stomach rolled. Ander had made her laugh.

That put him halfway home. More than halfway.

It wasn't right. Ander didn't need Stella the way Hagen did. Any woman would do for Ander. He'd be satisfied with anyone to throw an arm around as they settled in front of the television. Simplicity was all his friend needed.

But Stella was more.

She wasn't just beautiful, smart, and strong. She was the only person Hagen had met who understood his pain. Sure, she handled her struggles in her own way, but their path was the same. They shared something special, something Ander could never understand.

"Hey, listen." Ander's voice came back on the line. "Stella told me about her dad."

Hagen's fingers dug into Bubs's ribs. His dog let out a small yelp and leapt off the sofa. He huffed away and, for once, settled himself on his cushion.

"What did she tell you?"

"That she's trying to find the guy who ordered the dirty cops to have him killed. And you've been helping."

Hagen covered his eyes with a hand. "I have."

"That's great, man. Well done. But now you and Mac aren't alone anymore. You've got another pair of hands, and we're going to get him. As soon as we wrap up this case, we're going to crack that one too."

*Crack it. Sure. Like only cracking a case is going to be enough. It might be enough for Stella, but it would never be enough for me.*

He wasn't interested in solving the case. Or even closing it. He wanted to *complete* it.

"Let's crack this one first. We'll pick it up again tomorrow." He hung up and slid the phone onto the table.

On the flat-screen, Curry shimmied past a point guard.

Hagen stood up and strode to the end of the room.

Stella had brought Ander into their work. She'd expanded their circle, as if Mac being involved wasn't enough. He turned around and paced back to the window, his fists buried in his pockets.

*Doesn't matter.*

What difference did it make, how many people Stella involved? His focus wasn't on Stella. It had to be on finding his father's killer. And exacting revenge.

Ander. Mac. Stella. None of them mattered. Only vengeance.

## 27

Norm Connell wiped a bead of sweat from his forehead. Even though the hour was after ten thirty, the night's humidity kept him hot and damp. Moisture pooled in the folds of his ear as he sat on the porch of his bungalow. It was late to be organizing tomorrow's lighting gig, but Jake, his young assistant, was still struggling. Norm gave his instructions emphatically but quietly, because Kath didn't like noise late at night.

"We'll need the DMX snake, the box of truss grapples, and don't forget the Lycian. We can use the midget for this one."

A scratching came from the other end of the line as young Jake scribbled down what Norm said. The thought made Norm chuckle. He was a good kid, but he still had a lot to learn. He'd called to see if Norm would text the light list. Instead, Norm called him back and told him to write everything in longhand. He was old-fashioned that way. Jake would get used to it.

But it would do the kid good to write the names of the lighting gear. The more he interacted with those names, the easier it would be for him to remember them.

The scratching stopped. "The DMX, the truss apples, and what was the last one?"

Or not.

Norm sighed. "Grapples. The box of truss grapples and the midget Lycian. We'll use that for the spot."

The scratching restarted. Norm rested his can of beer against his temple. A drop of condensation ran past his sideburn and into his beard. It didn't help, and neither did the long draught he took immediately afterward. By the time he'd lowered the can, sweat had already re-formed on his brow. His shirt stuck to his back.

Through the half-open windows, Norm could see Kath lying on the sofa in front of her favorite show, a fan blowing her nightgown around her thighs.

Jake's voice sounded in his ear again, young and earnest. "What about the scoop lights? Clive said he didn't want them."

Norm rolled his eyes. Clive Taylor was the "talent"—a big description for a small-time singer who'd never sung his syrupy country ballads in an arena bigger than a school gym. Tomorrow wasn't going to be much better either. The park could barely hold little more than a hundred and fifty.

"We don't tell the talent what to sing, and they don't tell us what to light. They do their job, and we do ours. And our job is to make sure the audience can see what's happening on the stage. Pack the scoop lights. If Clive complains, tell him they're…dippers or something. He won't have a clue."

He took another sip of beer as Jake added the scoop lights to the equipment list.

A light struck the elm tree in front of the house, turning the trunk a pale shade of yellow. Norm frowned.

Goodlettsville was a quiet place. It was the kind of suburb where streets filled with traffic at eight, refilled at six, and were largely empty the rest of the time.

Especially where he lived.

His bungalow was the last on the street.

A car coming this far down the road was unusual and almost unheard of this time of night.

The driver was probably hunting for space to turn around.

Norm squinted through the trees. The headlights were weak. Those were old-school bulbs, not today's LEDs, and the lenses must have yellowed and fogged over the years.

The age of the car wasn't odd. The only thing stranger than seeing a moving vehicle down here this time of night was seeing a new one. No one on this street owned anything younger than a seven-year-old Ford.

The small sedan reached the end of the road, but instead of pulling a U-turn, the driver pulled up behind Norm's truck, stopping directly in front of the porch.

"Who the hell is that?" Behind Norm came a soft thump as Kath lowered her bare feet from the coffee table.

"Hey, Jake. I'll call you back, okay?"

Norm lowered his phone.

The car door opened, but the headlights remained on, casting an obscenely long shadow as the driver stepped into the light.

A pair of long legs.

The flap of a long jacket, hanging from the back like a tail.

A large head and the two long ears of a giant rabbit.

## 28

Stella slid the protein bar back across the conference table at the FBI's Resident Agency. "Not for me, thanks. Just had a chocolate chip cookie for breakfast."

Ander pulled the snack back to him. "Aw, you can't start your day with a cookie. You gotta stay healthy. Keep in shape. Breakfast is the most important meal of the day."

Hagen nudged him. "Then *you* have to do better than a health bar. Granola with açaí berries and oat milk. And a double shot of espresso. That's how someone should start the day."

"How *you* start the day. Normal folks wouldn't touch it. Ahchoo berries? Sounds like something you take for a cold."

Stella had to fight hard to hide her smile. Watching Ander tease Hagen was a better way to start the day than even a hot cocoa and a cookie.

Chloe reached across the table and pulled the protein bar from Ander's fingers.

"She doesn't want it? I'll have it."

As she slipped the bar into the bag hanging from the back of her chair, the door opened, and Slade entered.

Immediately, the atmosphere in the room changed. Gone was Ander's gentle ribbing. His attention was refocused on the crime, to the multiple corpses and a murderer on the loose.

Without speaking, Slade approached the whiteboard at the end of the room. Photographs of the five victims were already stuck to the board, arranged in one group of three and another group of two.

Next to each group, Slade added pictures of the crime scenes and drone shots of the estates' sprawling grounds. Stella recognized the victims' living rooms, the bodies bound to the chairs, and the partially eaten food on the Deems' dining room table.

Stella's chest tightened. There was often a moment in an investigation when the crime turned into a brain teaser, a mental challenge waiting to be cracked, like a crossword puzzle or sudoku.

But Slade wasn't merely laying out the facts of the case. He was reminding them what the case was about. Five people were dead. More might follow, and the victims deserved justice.

Slade turned from the board and placed the tips of his fingers on the top of the table, the way he always started a meeting.

"Right. Let's pull everything together. We've got two crime scenes and five victims. All the victims lived close to each other—"

Chloe interrupted. "You're saying they were all rich."

"I wasn't, Chloe, but they were." Slade shrugged, admitting the facts. "Both families were very wealthy. Donovan Freeman and his wife invested their wealth with Jeremy Deem, so the victims knew each other and mixed in the same circles."

"Including the philharmonic." Ander jabbed the end of a pen at the board.

"Fair point." Slade wrote *Kentwood Philharmonic* on the board and circled it. "Anyone else got anything to add?"

"The murder weapon." Hagen's hands curled into fists on the table, as though he were gripping something long and thin. "One of them, anyway. Ballistics is being run on the bullets, and the M.E. thinks the garrote is piano wire. The choice is strange and shows premeditation."

Slade added the two murder weapons, the gun and the wire, to the board.

The recurring piano element was bizarre, and Stella didn't believe in coincidences. Somehow, music was involved and probably central to this case.

"We've also got the video." Mac tapped her phone, pulling it up. "The clip links the victims together and connects them, again, to the philharmonic through Alice20. Tech is still working to lighten the video enough to allow facial recognition."

Slade took a deep breath. He wrote *Boris the Boringest* on the board, circled it, and linked the circle to the philharmonic and to the pictures of Jeremy Deem and Donovan Freeman.

This murder board was becoming stranger and stranger.

Slade jammed the cap back onto the marker and tossed it onto the table, as though he blamed the pen for the words he had to write.

"Any luck locating this Boris person?"

The room was silent. Stella lifted a pen. "We're still digging, sir. Boris has used the mononym for years, with all legal business paperwork and accounts in the singular name. He's a social media recluse at the best of times, and since that video appeared online, he hasn't been seen in public. Some forums theorize that he's killed himself."

Slade didn't appear pleased. "He wasn't born with one name, so keep digging."

Stella resisted the urge to say "duh," but nodded instead. "Yes, sir." She pushed two sheets of paper across the table. "I sent you the best images of this Boris person I could find online and printed a couple off. From all accounts, Boris is intensely shy and insisted his back be to the audience when he played. He shunned spotlights and preferred to move on and off stage in shadows. It's one of the reasons he was so sought after, I've gathered."

Slade posted the shadowed images of Boris's profile to the whiteboard. "You and Ander were at the philharmonic yesterday. What did you find?"

Stella sat up straighter. "Yeah, we spoke to Lisa Kerne. She's the pianist there, and she's Alice20, the one who left threats under the responses to the video."

The SSA grabbed the marker again. "Threats? And she knew the victims?"

He added *Lisa Kerne* to the board, placing it directly beneath the philharmonic.

Ander cleared his throat. "'Threats' might be a bit strong. She expressed anger at the audience for falling asleep during the performance. She knew Jeremy Deem, and it's possible she knew Donovan Freeman as well, but she was playing on the nights of both murders. Her alibi checks out. She's a strange one, though. Plays the piano like an angel but dresses like a goth, a real princess of darkness, and has a thing for *Alice in Wonderland*."

Chloe rolled her eyes. "If every eccentric musician was a murderer, every concert hall would be a crime scene, and every club would be the site of a massacre."

Hagen nodded. "Fair point. After all, we can't even judge FBI agents by their style. Can we, Chloe?"

Chloe pushed up the spikes of her cropped jet-black hair.

Hagen grinned.

Slade intervened. "Okay, that's enough. You're right, Chloe, but let's check her out. Stella, Ander, that's on you. Hagen, Chloe, I want you two to head back to Deem's office. But this time, we need Donovan Freeman's information. Maybe something else connects them, something we're missing." Slade's phone pinged. "Right, off you go. Back here as soon as you're done."

He pulled out his phone and scowled at the screen.

"Wait. Scrap that. Stay here."

Slade stepped out of the room. He was gone long enough for the team to exchange concerned glances. He'd gone pale when he returned. "We've got another murder."

Stella's stomach fell, as though an elevator had dropped from beneath her feet.

Last night, she and Ander had listened to a concert and enjoyed a drink. And while they'd sat there, the killer was out doing his thing.

She could have stopped him.

No. She couldn't have stopped him.

Of course she couldn't have. She wasn't inside his head. But she might have, if she'd been more diligent and less distracted.

Slade held up a hand as he read the report. "It's not in Kentwood."

Relief swept through Stella. She continued toward the door.

"But one of the victims appears to have been garroted. Stella, Ander, hold off on Lisa Kerne for now. I'll send you the details."

## 29

Stella wanted to believe the man on the porch was sleeping. If she squinted hard enough, she could imagine he was having a midmorning nap.

She pulled on her forensic suit. As soon as she zipped up, sweat prickled along her skin.

Norm Connell sat in a rocking chair. His legs were outstretched, his feet together. The back of his head rested against the top of the chair. One hand lay in the middle of his chest, as though he had dozed off while watching tufts of clouds drift across the blue sky.

But to believe he was asleep meant ignoring the red stain soaking the top of his shirt, the spray of blood that left a line of dots up the window, and the wide gap around his throat. None of those were easy to overlook.

Stella pulled on her hood. "He certainly looks like one of ours, doesn't he?"

Ander snapped a glove on, tugging on the fingers. Stella didn't envy Ander's height and weight in these suits. The latex gloves were uncomfortable enough for her, tight and sweaty at the same time. She'd hate to know what they were like on the hands of a six-four guy.

He tilted his head and sized the victim up. "Not exactly in Kentwood, though, are we?"

Holding on to the edges of her hood, Stella peered around the lawn. This certainly wasn't Kentwood. Not even close.

The houses weren't dilapidated trailers or clapboard slums, but they also weren't the Deems' or Freemans' giant McMansions.

The neighborhood was made up mostly of one- or two-bedroom bungalows. A couple of drives held old pickups hoisted on jacks, waiting for repairs that would never come.

Front lawns were unkempt, and a few held children's toys left to bleach in the sun. Stella doubted they were going to find any salmon and asparagus dinners in these houses prepared by pro chefs, let alone a grand piano.

"No, we're not in Kentwood. You ready?"

Ander nodded, and Stella led him under the police tape. As they climbed the stairs leading up to the porch, the front door opened.

The officer who came out was short with high, round cheeks and wide hips. Her hood was down, and her short locks were tied back.

"Grace Shipman, investigating officer. They told me the FBI would be coming round here. Didn't tell me what for, though."

She didn't offer her hand, which suited Stella. Trying to shake in latex gloves was like trying to take a bath in a bedsheet. Never a comfortable experience and hardly worth it.

Grace noticed Ander, who took the investigating officer's lead and lowered his own hood. As his curls freed themselves from his suit, her eyes widened.

They narrowed again when she turned her attention back to Stella.

"We're just talking about a local crime. Nothing to bother the FBI about." She threw an arm wide, taking in the surrounding houses. "We got some rough neighborhoods around here. We probably get a couple of nasty homicides every year. First time I've ever seen the FBI show an interest."

Stella gave her a small nod. "Guess this time you got lucky. Landed yourself something connected to an ongoing investigation."

She stepped past Officer Shipman and through the open door.

A photographer paused as Stella came in but said nothing. He raised his camera and took another shot of a living room that seemed frozen in time. A tall gooseneck lamp threw a spotlight onto a glass corner table covered with bottles of tequila, rum, and bourbon. A coffee table held a small pile of opened letters and a remote control. By the half-open window, the leaves of a ficus plant were browning.

But apart from Stella and the photographer, the only thing moving was a celebrity chef on the forty-inch television screen. He explained how to make the perfect soufflé to a room where no one was interested or had much of an appetite.

Certainly, the middle-aged woman sprawled on the sofa wasn't hungry. One arm was pinned between her side and the cushion. One leg stretched along the sofa, and the other draped off the side, as though she'd been shot in the face just as she was getting up.

The bullet had struck her between the eyebrow and the eyeball. The entire side of her face was covered in blood. What had once been an eye socket was now a dark hole.

The photographer crouched next to Stella and snapped a picture. The flash blasted a sterile white light into the room.

"Definitely no piano." Ander joined her next to the table, his gaze fixed on the female victim.

Grace Shipman stopped in the doorway, her hands on her hips. "Piano? Agents, if you're looking for someone who drops pianos on people, you really are in the wrong place. I told you. This is a regular robbery gone wrong. Happens all the time."

"I'm sure it does." Stella took a deep breath, trying to keep her patience. "But when I was a cop, if someone broke into a house and killed the owners, I wouldn't expect to see a giant television still on the wall. And I certainly wouldn't expect to see three bottles of liquor untouched on a table."

The investigating officer rocked on her heels. "Were probably disturbed before they could load their stash. The shot is probably what did it. Didn't expect to fire the gun, and when they did, they were out of here like turds from a sick goose."

"What can you tell us about the victims?"

"The guy outside is Norm Connell."

"What else you got?"

"He's a lighting director. Works at events and small shows and so on. This is his wife, Kath. Preschool teacher. The kids aren't even old enough to hate her yet."

Ander glanced at Stella. "Profile's wrong too. This is a Working Joe, not some rich dude."

Stella nodded. "The MO is right, though. Garroting and shooting. Don't see that combo too often."

She leaned over the table and peered down at the victim. A mark on the wall showed where the bullet had passed in through the half-open front window and then out the back of the woman's skull, spraying her brains across the wallpaper. She must have been middle-aged, about the same age as

Donovan Freeman and his wife. Like the others, she'd been murdered in her own home, in a place she thought was safer than any other.

Stella would bet good money that the bullet they recovered was a 9 mm. At least they could have ballistics see if it matched the previous shootings.

There was nothing else to see here, no half-eaten meals and no security footage showing rabbit-headed intruders. There was too little here worth stealing.

Stella turned and strode back to the porch. As she lowered her hood and peeled off her gloves, she took a deep breath of fresh air.

Ander joined her. "What do you think?"

Stella unzipped her Tyvek suit, her back to the house. She scrunched it up and dropped it in the hands of a tech waiting next to the steps of the porch.

"Not sure. Big difference between this place and Kentwood. But the methods are too similar to ignore."

Ander ran a hand through his curls. "What's the link, though?"

Stella studied the house, remembering everything the investigator said. "Norm Connell worked in lighting, right?"

Ander nodded. "And concerts need special lighting."

Chewing her lips, Stella made a decision. "Let's send images of the Connells to Mac to see if one or both were in the Boris audience that night."

Ander snorted. "Think she can use her magical powers to spot bone structure through a dimly lit room?"

Stella shrugged. "Facial recognition has come a long way, so maybe. In the meantime, let's go and talk to Lisa Kerne again. If she knew him, we'll have a connection."

## 30

As Hagen exited the elevator on the ninth floor, the *Deem Finance* sign greeted him once again. Chloe touched his back and slipped past him into the office. Hagen followed, letting the door swing closed behind them.

There was little sign the company's leader had recently died. Each cubicle appeared full. The room hummed with quiet conversation. Keyboard clicking sounded out like snare drums.

The receptionist counter was empty, though. They waited for someone to greet them. And waited.

"Screw this," Hagen grumbled and headed in the direction of Karen Neuglass's office.

Outside her door, he knocked on the frame, but Karen's helmet of curly orange hair didn't lift as she continued typing.

*Is she hard of hearing or simply ignoring our presence?*

When Hagen cleared his throat, Karen lifted a finger and continued typing for another full minute. With a loud sigh, she finally acknowledged them.

"Yes?"

One side effect of working for the FBI was few people were pleased to see an agent at their door. Either they were suspects about to get a grilling, or they were witnesses forced to relive a trauma.

Hagen's job was always to fire up the heat or to pick at the scab.

Neither made him particularly welcome.

Hagen stepped into the office. He spoke quietly, trying to keep his words from drifting to the cubicles down the hall. "We need some information about Donovan Freeman."

Karen pushed her glasses to the bottom of her nose. She scrutinized Hagen as though she were talking to an employee stepping out of line. The glasses made her look like an old schoolmarm. No wonder she didn't always wear them. Contacts, anyone?

"Mr. Freeman? What on earth would you want to know about him for?"

Hagen glanced at Chloe. Clearly, word hadn't spread yet. Chief Gray must have been doing a pretty good job of keeping a lid on things.

Chloe leaned against the doorframe. "Is there somewhere we can talk privately?"

"Well, I suppose we *could* use Mr. Deem's office. Mr. Deem…Jem…hasn't taken over his position yet."

Karen led them back through the corridor to the late Mr. Deem's office. Nothing had changed since they'd last visited, which was impressive to Hagen. Even the first crime scene hadn't remained untouched.

The desk was still empty. The television was still dark, and the books undisturbed. The place reminded Hagen of a museum display. As much as he distrusted Jem, Hagen hoped Jeremy's son would start working here soon, if only to sweep away the sense of emptiness filling the space.

Karen closed the door behind her. "Now, why do you want to know about Donovan Freeman?"

Hagen gave himself a moment to think through his explanation. Chief Gray clearly didn't want to frighten the residents of Kentwood. But he needed Karen Neuglass's cooperation.

"Because he's dead. Murdered. Probably by the same person who killed Jeremy Deem and his family."

Karen slapped her hand to her chest. "Oh, my lord. How awful. When will this end?"

Chloe leaned a hip against the edge of the desk and folded her arms. "When we catch the murderer. And the more you help us, the sooner that will be."

Karen swallowed. "Well…what do you want to know? He was a very nice man. He was one of Mr. Deem's best clients. He took him on, oh, must be about five years ago now."

"Do you know how they met?"

"I think it was at the philharmonic. Mr. Freeman was a regular, and they got to talking during one of the intermissions, I believe. You know, of course, Mr. Deem was a huge supporter of the arts."

"We know."

"Can we see his file?" Hagen pointed at the computer, the only item on Jeremy Deem's desk.

Karen straightened her shoulders. "You wish to look at his finances? I think you'll need to ask his wife first. I couldn't possibly—"

"She's dead too."

Karen's mouth hung open for a moment. Eventually, her hand rose to cover her lips. "My lord."

Chloe pushed the monitor around and picked up the wireless keyboard. "They didn't have any children, so there are no heirs we can ask. And we have a warrant." She pulled the tri-folded paper from her back pocket.

Slade had gotten all the paperwork done sometime in the middle of the night. Even though Slade sent him to autopsies, Hagen admired the man. His boss was relentless.

Karen sat at the keyboard and stared at the monitor. After a second, she seemed to remember where she was and what she was doing. She swiveled the monitor so everyone could see.

"No, they wouldn't have any heirs. I understand they planned to leave almost everything to the philharmonic. Mr. Deem had talked to them about it. He was intent their money go to a good cause in the event…in the event…"

She sniffed and blew her nose on a tissue.

"I'm so sorry. Excuse me. Here." She typed. "This is their account. Mr. Deem managed it himself."

The screen populated with numbers and initials, lists of shares and funds where Jeremy Deem had put his client's money.

Financial forensics wasn't Hagen's field, though he sometimes wondered whether he shouldn't have specialized in it. His father had often told him about the complicated steps his shady clients would take to protect their wealth. Following the money wasn't as much fun as following suspects down dark alleys, but it often led to much faster results.

He scrolled down the page. Chloe rested her elbows on the desk beside him.

The list of initials and numbers stretched on. Two hundred thousand dollars here, a few million dollars there. Each investment held more money than Hagen would earn in his career.

He'd never felt poor, although since paying cash for his home, the numbers in his bank account had been uncomfortably low. But seeing the size of these investments boggled his mind. The numbers made him feel small, as though he were barely even trying.

Chloe frowned, and Hagen wanted to chuckle at the puzzled look on her face. Chloe's specialties involved kicking people in the face. Money matters didn't actually *matter* to her. "Anything?"

"Not really. Wait…" Hagen stopped scrolling.

Freeman had put three million dollars in an account called the New Note Trust Fund.

He highlighted the fund and turned the monitor to Karen. "What's this?"

The admin pushed her glasses against the bridge of her nose and peered over his shoulder. "Oh, that's a trust fund."

"I can see that. What's it for?"

Karen took a deep breath. "It was set up about five years ago. The money provides funds to up-and-coming musicians over the span of five years. They can develop their talent during that time without having to worry about money. Some of them are very poor, you know."

"Musicians?" Chloe straightened, her interest piqued.

Hagen reviewed the fund's goals. "The recipients are provided room and board and an additional three thousand dollars per month for other expenses." He whistled. That was a generous trust indeed.

Karen beamed at him. "Yes. Without any financial strain, the artists could focus on their works. I thought it was a brilliant idea."

Hagen pushed the keyboard toward Karen. "Can you show us the beneficiaries?"

Karen brought up a spreadsheet. There were half a dozen names on the sheet.

The first name on the list was Lisa Kerne.

## 31

With only one music store in town, I had little choice. G-Clef Instruments was part of the Main Street strip mall. When I stepped inside, the world became fluorescent and fake.

While there was a display "window" filled with guitars, the display was enclosed. No actual windows allowed any natural light inside. It took my eyes a moment to adjust.

Though, at the end of the day, I didn't need light. I could play a piano blindfolded. And I needed to play today. It had been too long.

The piano stood on a platform near the center of the music store. Its lid was propped open, allowing customers to watch the hammers hit the strings. The store allowed anyone to play, even rug rats who beat the keys with no respect for melody.

Once upon a time, I'd played in auditoriums across Europe.

I had filled the most beautiful halls in the world.

Now, I had to be content with a music store display piano in a small Tennessean town.

How the mighty had fallen.

I sat on the stool and flexed my fingers.

*The things I could do to an instrument like this.*

Without even looking, I let my fingers drift onto the keys. Ravel's *Pavane for a Dead Princess*. I always warmed up with Ravel.

I closed my eyes as the notes fell from my fingertips like raindrops on the petals of a rose. Such a shame there was no one to hear them. Or almost no one. I could hardly count the store assistant and the customer searching for a new electric guitar strap as an audience. They moved about their business as if I didn't exist.

The piano was indeed as young and spritely as I'd expected it to be. I didn't want to stop. The store might not have had the acoustics of a music hall, but hearing music, real music, was enough. Finally.

I turned in my seat and addressed my audience of two. "Chopin's Nocturne op. 9, no. 2."

The store assistant and his guitar-strap-buying customer shared a look.

I ignored their ignorance and turned my attention to Chopin. I didn't need sheet music. The notes were ingrained in my heart. Nocturne op. 9, no. 2 was part of every solo performance I'd ever given.

My fingers did the work.

Eventually, the store manager would kick me out, despite the fact he should have been paying me to play there.

But while I had access to that piano, I would savor each note.

I played and played, and no one bothered me for almost an hour. Customers came and went. And I forgot everything. My list of names flew away. The wire stashed under the passenger seat of my car vanished. The gun next to it faded. The mask and morning suit were forgotten. All the misery and wretchedness of the last three years were buried under the beautiful imagination of Frédéric François Chopin.

"It's him, isn't it?"

The voice, a jarring, nasal bleat, came from behind me.

An answering snigger, like a jackal, vibrated the air.

A shudder passed through me. I tried to ignore them.

The first person tried again. "It is. I'm telling you, it's him. Look. It's the same hair and same suit."

"Man, it might be."

*As hard as I tried, would I never escape the peanut gallery?*

I played on. I had to play on.

Both voices were young and whiny. I wouldn't have put them beyond their late teens.

"Go on. Ask him."

"No. You ask him!"

There was the sound of a shove, then footsteps approaching from behind. A giggle.

I braced myself. My hour of peace was at an end.

"Excuse me."

I lifted my fingers from the keyboard. I didn't turn around.

"Yes?"

"Are you the man in this video?" He shoved his phone under my nose. Laughter came from behind me, where his companion waited. "This one where everyone fell asleep?"

A wave of red-hot lava seared down my spine. I spun on the stool, and the youth—because it was, as I suspected, a teenage boy, spotty-faced and greasy-haired—stepped back, almost falling off the piano platform.

"Philistine! You ignorant, stupid, little boy. I will—"

My hands curled into fists. I could have throttled him. If my piano wire and gun had only been in my pocket, I would have strangled him then and there and shot his companion right between the eyes.

I stormed out of the store, their laughter and their snoring sounds following me outside. My fury hadn't eased by the time I opened my car door.

Overwhelmed by indecision and shame, I did the only thing I could think of...placed a call.

"I told you to never call me." The hissed words were like alcohol poured over my weeping wounds.

I closed my eyes to block out the censure and shared my latest experience. My greatest supporter would surely understand.

"Ah. Yes, I see. How terribly dreadful that must have been for you."

I ran a hand under my nose, appalled by the tears and snot falling out of me. "It was."

"I have an idea, but it would be risky, combining the climax and finale into one."

The finale? The idea of this being over was peaceful.

"I'd like that very much."

"Do you know who you want to make sleep forever?"

I brought out my list and found the name. "Yes."

"Good. Then do everything I say."

## 32

From the road, Lisa Kerne's house in East Nashville appeared small and unassuming. Squares of concrete formed a small driveway. A compact, older-model Honda was parked at the end of the drive, facing the street.

The lawn was neatly cut. The siding on the house was a lighter shade of gray than the roof slates. Three windows looked out over the street, and the house didn't appear to be more than a single room deep.

Stella closed the passenger door behind her and waited for Ander to catch up.

"Looks like she's home."

Ander locked the car. "I'm guessing she's home alone too. This place is too small for a family. Must be a single bedroom."

Stella strode up the drive. As she passed the Honda, she peered through the window. The car might have been old, but its interior appeared new. There was no cup in the cupholder, no tissues or candy wrappers stuffed into the door pockets. Even the rubber mat in front of the passenger seat shone.

Ander peeked past Stella's shoulder. "Wish my car was that clean."

"You could, you know, wash it on occasion."

Ander shook his head and bounded past her toward the front door. "Too much effort. And I want Murphy to feel at home when he comes down to visit. Don't want him to feel he can't touch anything because it's too clean, you know?"

Stella followed him onto the small porch and rang the doorbell. "I think that's the worst excuse I've ever heard for living like a slob."

"I don't live like a slob. How would you even know? You haven't been to my place." Ander leaned against a porch pillar. "We get this thing done, and I'll have a dinner party. Well, maybe a barbeque. Okay, I'll order takeout and invite a bunch of people over. You'll see how house-trained I—"

The door opened, and Ander faced the woman glaring at them.

Still in head-to-toe black, today's ensemble consisted of a pair of sweats and a tight tank top. Lisa Kerne's black hair was pushed to one side, exposing the shaved stripe above her ear. Without makeup, her face was even paler than it had been at the philharmonic.

She sighed. "I remember you two. What do you want?"

Stella offered a friendly smile, hoping to head off a bit of Lisa's attitude. "Mind if we come in? We've got a few more questions for you, and it's kind of hot out here." She fanned her face for emphasis.

Lisa stood in the doorway, one arm blocking the way.

After a second, she shrugged and moved aside.

Stella stepped into the house and stifled a gasp.

The wall was covered in large lilac-and-white diamonds. The floor tiles were a giant chessboard. Checkered squares angled across the house. Two green velvet armchairs stood under a row of shelves covered with dolls of Alice, the

Cheshire Cat, the White Rabbit, and the Queen of Hearts. The Mad Hatter, interestingly enough, wasn't present.

*We're all quite mad here. You'll fit right in.*

Keeping one eye on Lisa Kerne, Stella took in the rest of the busy room. Dominating the space was a petit grand piano. But even the piano stool was topped with a cushion showing Alice surrounded by flowers and a motto urging her to *paint the flowers red.*

There was no television, no couch, and no real creature comforts. Despite the bright characters, Lisa Kerne appeared to live like some kind of musical monk.

The floor pattern almost made Stella nauseous. The house was like an overly designed escape room, the sort of place you'd pull down shelves to find the key to leave. How someone could live here, let alone enjoy living here, was beyond her.

Lisa adjusted the cushion, sat down, and started playing scales.

Stella, for the first time in a while, was speechless.

Ander managed to find a sentence. "You really do like *Alice in Wonderland*, don't you?"

Lisa ran her fingers up the keys. "Is that what you came here to ask?"

"No." Stella pulled herself together. She kept her eyes focused on Lisa. The number of checkered patterns—on the wall and on the floor—was making her dizzy. "Norm Connell. Do you know him?"

Lisa shook her head. "Should I?"

"I don't know. He's a lighting director. You ever met him?"

"Not as far as I know. But I don't really talk to the techs."

Ander's phone rang, smothering the light tinkle of Lisa's piano with a loud declaration of love for rock and roll. "Sorry." He took the call and disappeared onto the porch. While he was gone, Stella debated what question she should follow with, but Ander returned almost instantly, his face dark.

The call must have been from one of the team, Slade or Hagen. He had something.

Ander stopped in the middle of the room, both feet planted on black squares.

"Lisa, yesterday we asked you about Donovan Freeman."

Lisa shrugged again. Her fingers continued stroking the keys. "I really don't remember."

"I do. You said you didn't know him. We had to remind you he was a subscriber to your philharmonic. He was also in the video under which you placed a threatening message."

"For the last time, it wasn't a threatening message. I just thought they deserved to die."

Stella's eyebrows rose. "That's not a threat?"

"No. It's an opinion." Lisa played a minor chord and held it.

"Can you stop playing for a moment, please?"

That was the closest to angry Stella had ever heard Ander.

"Why didn't you tell us Donovan Freeman gave you thirty thousand dollars?"

Stella's eyes widened. Ander was direct. But she recovered fast enough to add pressure to Lisa. "That's quite the omission."

Lisa struck another chord. "I don't know what you're talking about."

Ander gritted his teeth. If the piano had an electrical cord, Stella was sure he would have yanked it out of the wall by now. "You've received over a hundred thousand dollars from the New Note Trust Fund over the last three years."

"So? It's a special award for young musicians."

"The trust was funded by Donovan Freeman."

Lisa's fingers stopped above the keyboard. She pulled them back toward her and held them in her lap.

"Is that so? Well, Agent, I have to tell you. I *still* don't know Donovan Freeman. The philharmonic suggested I apply to the fund. So I filled in the forms, and wow, wow, wow! I won. Where the money comes from, I don't know." She lowered her voice and turned to them directly. "Although, I'm starting to think it's a shame he died. The killer certainly didn't do me any favors, did he? What with *killing my sponsor*."

Stella had had enough. "Lisa, we've got a morgue filling up with bodies. You threatened two of them and took money from another. It's possible Donovan Freeman's death will free up more money for musicians like you. But every time we ask you about those victims, you shrug and act like you don't know or care."

Lisa tilted her head and looked directly into Stella's eyes. "What's your name?"

"Knox. Stella Knox."

"Agent Knox, Stella Knox, I have to tell you, as soon as you walk out of here, I'm going to forget your name. The people I meet, I don't really care about. I like music. I like books...well, two books in particular. Everything else doesn't really interest me. And I'm afraid *everything else* includes both of you."

Stella tried to process Lisa's coldness. The woman was like ice. Stella couldn't remember ever meeting anyone as disinterested in the world as Lisa Kerne.

They weren't going to get anything more out of her.

Unless they wanted to know about Bach's concertos or something to do with *Alice in Wonderland*, Lisa wasn't going to be much help.

Finally, Stella managed to find her voice. "Thank you for your time, Ms. Kerne."

As Stella followed Ander back to the door, she slowed.

The Queen of Hearts watched her from the end of the shelf, the doll's long, red train trailing toward the floor.

Stella stopped. "Lisa, what *is* this thing with you and *Alice in Wonderland*? I mean, don't you think this is all a bit much?"

"A bit much?" She leaned forward, her hands still folded in her lap. "I suppose I shouldn't have expected more from FBI agents. If you don't understand the power of music to move people, how would you understand this?"

Ander stood in the doorway. In another moment, he'd be dragging her out of this madhouse.

Still, Stella persisted. "Understand what? Try me."

Lisa fixed her gaze on Stella. "My mother began reading Lewis Carroll's novels to me before she fell ill. After she died, my father carried on. He finished *Through the Looking Glass*, and I asked him to start again. He did. Going back to the nonsense world reminded both of us of my mom. Every night, he'd read me a chapter. And if he was away at a performance or on tour, I'd recall the chapter from memory. I know both books by heart. 'Alice was beginning to get very tired of sitting by her sister on the bank and—'"

Stella held up a hand. "Wait. At a performance? On tour?"

"Yes. My father's a musician. A pianist. He taught me everything I know. Dad traveled a lot. Went all around the world giving concerts. I had to look after myself while he was on the road, but I had a lot of time to practice. And to read."

*A pianist. Her father was a pianist.*

"Lisa, what's your dad's name?"

Lisa bounced her finger on middle C. The note reverberated through the room. "Boris."

Stella murmured to herself. "Boris the Boringest."

"Yes." That phrase turned Lisa's coldness into a vicious heat. Her voice was sharp, angry. "Boris the *Boringest*. Those idiots. I hated to see him humiliated. He didn't deserve it."

Stella breathed in slowly. Now she understood. "Boris the Boringest" was Lisa's father. This wasn't about this young woman.

The case was about her father.

The conniving little bitch had omitted that nugget of information during their previous conversation.

Stella pulled out her phone and opened the video.

There was Jeremy Deem, and there was Donovan Freeman. She scrolled forward to the last frames.

And there, barely visible against the wall, with one hand on the light stand, was a dark figure too blurry to recognize. Was that Norm Connell?

If so, the video connected every victim. They needed a clearer version of the video pronto.

"What happened to your dad? After the video, where did he go?"

Lisa turned back to the piano and began playing again. The room filled with sharp, staccato notes.

"He disappeared for a while. I hardly heard from him for almost three years. He said he was staying in a beach house somewhere, but he didn't tell me where."

"A beach house? He's still there now?"

Lisa shook her head. She played on. Stella waited for Lisa to respond, but the musician had dismissed her.

"Lisa, where's your father now?"

The pianist closed her eyes. Her head fell against her shoulder as she let the music take her away. "He called me a few weeks ago. I thought he'd died, but he was here, staying at the Kentwood Motel. I asked if he wanted me to put him up, but he said he had a few things to do first." Lisa opened her eyes and smiled at Stella. "It's good to have him back."

Stella and Ander took their exit cue.

By the time they'd reached the car, she was already on the phone with Slade.

## 33

Hagen stood outside room 217 of the Kentwood Motel and knocked hard on the door. The flimsy material shook from his pounding.

The motel, next to the overpass near the town's industrial area, had fewer than thirty rooms.

Every surface—the planters with their dead vegetation, the handrail of the outside stairs leading up to the second floor, the ledges of every window—was covered with thick layers of gray powder. The air smelled of cement dust with a hint of old ash. Standing on the balcony above the parking lot made Hagen feel dirty.

He knocked again and shouted, "Boris Kerne. This is the FBI. Open up!"

Still, there was no answer.

"He's not in there?"

A housekeeper was standing down the exterior concrete passageway. A pile of yellowish bedsheets hid the bottom half of her face.

Chloe took a few steps down the passage to the cleaning woman. "Do you know where he's gone?"

The woman jammed the sheets into the basket on her cart. "No idea. Surprised he's not there, though. Hardly ever leaves his room. Every time I come up here, he's got his *Do Not Disturb* sign on the door. Plays his music real loud too."

Hagen swore quietly. He beat his fist twice on the door, making it rattle in its frame.

Slade had dispatched Hagen and Chloe to the motel because they were the closest.

Stella and Ander had managed to get a location for the guy in the piano video. Unlike his daughter, Lisa, Boris had no alibi yet, and a motive.

Hagen didn't know if he admired or pitied Boris if he was, indeed, killing off the people who'd slept through his performance. Hagen understood the need for revenge, but this seemed a petty sort of vengeance.

Quite a few people had been in attendance at the private performance.

If Boris Kerne intended to kill them all, he'd need a great deal of determination. And a lot of hate.

They'd need to act fast to stop him.

Chloe grabbed his shoulder. "Doesn't look like he's here, does it?"

"No. Any news on the search warrant?"

Chloe checked her phone and shook her head. "Slade said he'll do what he can, but it's not very likely, is it? Not yet, anyway."

"Dammit."

Hagen whirled away from the uncooperative door. He gripped the handrail and peered down at the near-empty parking lot. When he let go, his fingers and palms were covered with gray dust. He swore again and clapped his hands, puffing up a small cloud.

Chloe nodded toward the Explorer parked directly

beneath them. It looked like a behemoth next to his shiny Corvette. "Wait him out?"

"He could be all day. We still don't know if there's anything to him. He could be here to see his daughter, and that's it."

Chloe jerked her head toward the housekeeper. "She's got a key."

He'd already thought of that. It was a risk. A search without a warrant or probable cause could get their case tossed out in court. Still...

"Do we risk it?"

Chloe appeared conflicted too. "Dammit." She cupped her hands on the window glass and tried to peer inside. "Curtain's drawn. Can't see a damn thing."

She pulled back and headed toward the stairs.

"Is that a no?"

Chloe threw up her hands. "Come on. We'll wait for him. Haven't done a stakeout for a while. Stella and Ander are on their way. We can figure out a rotation and order some donuts. Your treat."

The housekeeper pushed her cart toward them, stopping next to room 215. She reached into her pocket for her key card.

"Chloe, just a second." Hagen turned to the housekeeper. "Can you do this one next?" He tapped the door of Boris Kerne's room.

"Why?"

"Does it matter to you? May as well do it while he's out, eh? No *Do Not Disturb* on the doorknob now."

The housekeeper shrugged. She had heavy shoulders, rounded by years of pushing a cart, dragging a vacuum cleaner, and scrubbing the insides of toilet bowls.

She jammed the key card into the slot and pushed the

door open. As she reached for her cart, Hagen stood in front of the doorway and peered inside.

The room was dark and smelled of unwashed clothes, mold, and sewage—the same odors leaking out of all the rooms in the motel.

Clothes poured out of a small, open suitcase at the foot of the bed. The sheets were mildly disturbed, as though Boris Kerne had thought of making the bed but had given up without finishing the task.

On a table by the wall, next to a crumpled white shirt, lay a copy of *Alice in Wonderland*. The edges of the pages had grayed with use. The corners bent upward. A white rabbit commanded the cover. The animal wore a tunic covered in hearts, blew a trumpet, and held a scroll. His ears stuck up sharply.

Hagen took a deep breath. The housekeeper came closer. She was holding an armful of clean towels. Hagen held up a hand. "Just a second."

He kept his toes behind the entrance but leaned into the doorway. A black jacket hung on a hook on the wall. Its long tails stretched almost to the floor. On the floor next to the bed, barely visible, two red dots the size of dimes stained the old, thin carpet.

"Chloe! Get up here. Looks like we've got blood."

The housekeeper froze. She dumped the towels back onto her cart and rammed her fists onto her hips. "I'm not cleaning no blood. Uh-uh."

Chloe pushed past her. "Please don't. This room is off limits now." She peered into the room. "We've got ourselves a nest. Any sign of the murder weapons?"

Hagen crouched and tried to see under the bed. "Can't see anything. Could be hidden in there somewhere, though."

"Or he might have them with him and already be on his way to his next victims."

"That's a nice thought."

"I'll call it in."

As Chloe called Slade, listing their probable cause for a warrant, Hagen leaned over the balcony.

Ander's car pulled into the lot and drew up next to the Explorer.

Hagen waved them up.

Stella arrived first, greeting Chloe with a squeeze of her upper arm before squinting into the motel room.

"What have we got?"

Hagen watched Ander take the stairs two at a time. "Looks like the killer's hole."

"Really?"

"Maybe. Sure looks like it. But he's not home. Could be out killing right now as we stand here."

Stella shook her head, sending her ponytail waving. "He hasn't killed during the day. But he might be scouting."

Ander groaned as he leaned against the brick exterior. "If we knew who he was after, we could be more proactive."

"Maybe we can figure it out."

Hagen glanced at Stella. "How?"

Stella pulled out her phone and called Mac, hitting the speaker button so they could all hear. "Any luck on rendering the audience in the Boris video more clearly?"

"Yeah. Quite a bit, actually. We couldn't do anything about the faces not in the frames, obviously, or faces blocked by other participants. But we were able to brighten the shot and use AI to assume the facial features. They might not be one hundred percent, but they should prove helpful."

Stella shot a thumbs-up. "Fantastic, because I really could use it now."

"Hold on."

A few seconds later, Stella's phone vibrated, and she clicked the notification. "Got it, Mac. Thanks."

"We'll keep working on it, and I'll send further updates as I can."

"You're the best."

Hagen held his breath as she disconnected the call and opened the newly rendered Boris performance.

"Wow." Hagen drew close enough to peer over her shoulder. "Much better."

Stella nodded. "Yeah."

It really was.

"There's Jeremy Deem and Donovan Freeman." She expanded the screen to show behind the spotlight. A dim reflection revealed a middle-aged, balding man holding a light stand. "Is that Norm Connell?"

Hagen held up his phone next to hers, and they compared the video image to the photograph of Connell's driver's license.

"Yeah, I think so."

"So if Boris is our man, whoever's next is probably in this video." Hagen stepped back and rested his hands on the balcony rail, thinking through their next steps. Slade had assigned Stella and Ander to work together on this case, so as much as he hated for them to be teamed up, it would be better to not shake that tree right then. "Maybe someone at the philharmonic can recognize the others. Why don't you two head there? We'll wait here for forensics and see if our rabbit pops his head back into his hole."

## 34

The concert hall of the Kentwood Philharmonic was loud—and not from music. Stella was tempted to cup her hands over her ears as a drill screamed outside an office wall. A nail gun beat out a rhythm from another nearby office. A man in a fluorescent vest shouted in Spanish into his phone.

A receptionist sat at a computer behind an unfinished half wall, headphones covering her ears. She had a pained expression on her face.

Stella approached and tapped on the surface of her desk. The woman lowered her headphones. Somewhere in the office corridor, a sheet of metal screeched. The woman winced, but her gaze passed from Stella to Ander and remained there.

For a moment, the pain seemed to pass from her face. Another victim of the Ander Effect.

Stella brought out her ID. "Where can we find Amy Cooper?"

The woman skimmed the card, then she shook her head and shouted, "Can you speak up? This place is deafening."

Ander swiped a lock of hair from his cheek and lowered his face close to her ear. She relaxed, as if the noise and chaos had vanished into thin air.

"Amy Cooper. Where can we find her?"

"She's out back. Quieter out there."

Stella thanked her and led Ander through the construction in the corridor and out through a fire door to a small courtyard behind the concert hall. The stone patio was large enough to hold a small bar and half a dozen high tables for chatting and drinking. The philharmonic probably charged a small fortune for holding corporate events and second weddings here.

Amy Cooper sat at one end of a cane sofa in the shade of the far wall. At the other end of the sofa sat an elderly man in a gray suit. Despite the heat, he wore a sports jacket. But he'd removed his tie and opened the top two buttons of his white shirt. His white hair was neatly combed. One leg was casually crossed over the other, revealing a long stretch of dark gray sock above a brown leather shoe.

For a moment, Stella wondered whether this was how Hagen might dress one day. If he invested wisely, managed his money, and could shove the chip off his shoulder.

Or maybe this was how his father would have turned out had he lived.

As they approached, Amy touched the man's arm and whispered something Stella couldn't quite hear. She lifted her other hand, telling Stella and Ander to stay where they were.

Stella ignored her request.

She was in no mood to wait for Amy Cooper.

Somewhere out there, Boris was probably hunting for his next victim. The philharmonic could wait.

Amy stood up. "If you wouldn't mind waiting, I'll be with

y'all in a moment." She lowered her voice. "Mr. Barr is a very important donor—"

Stella cut her off. "Ms. Cooper, the FBI is currently investigating the murders of a number of individuals associated with the Kentwood Philharmonic. We need your help to focus our investigation. If you don't help us now, we'll have to dig into the finances of everyone associated with the orchestra, including all its donors."

Mr. Barr chuckled, seemingly amused. He stood up and patted Amy on the shoulder. "Understood, Agent. Amy, we'll talk later." With a flash of glittering white teeth, he passed Stella and Ander and headed back into the concert hall.

Stella pulled up the video on her phone.

Ander met Amy's hard expression with a grin. But Amy was beyond the Ander Effect. "We need your help to identify people in this video. Shouldn't take long."

Amy gritted her teeth.

Stella found the video and turned the phone toward Amy.

Her face fell. "Oh, this thing? Why are you people looking at this? You don't think this performance had anything to do with..." She saw their expressions. "Oh, good heavens. You think it does." Her hand rose to her mouth.

Stella pressed the pause button. "You know this video?"

"Of course I know this video. Everyone in the classical music world does." Amy lowered her hand, sighing. "Poor Jeremy. He paid for this concert as a treat for his clients. Flew everyone out there. His own wife and her mother were there, you know?"

Stella looked at the paused screen. She didn't see Margaret Taylor, and there was only a glimpse of Penny Deem's floral shoulder. The video didn't show everyone.

"Right. We've tried to get in touch with the Budapest Philharmonic about the event, but the woman in charge of these things is on vacation. They're trying to reach her." Dammit. They needed that information.

Amy shrugged, as if it were no big deal. "Once you've chartered the jet, you may as well fill it, right? He took a bunch of clients, but he also took a few local officials. Never hurts to build connections, you know? He didn't plan very well, though. He booked Boris to play the same night they arrived. They went straight from the airport to the concert hall after a thirteen-hour flight. If they'd eaten and had any alcohol at all, it's not surprising they all fell asleep."

"Yeah, I guess even the noise in there wouldn't keep me awake after a thirteen-hour flight." Stella tilted her head toward the construction cacophony behind them. "Can you name the people in the audience?"

"I don't know. If memory serves, it was very dark and—"

"The video's been rendered for quality."

Amy sighed. "I'll try." She called off names as Stella dragged the video onward. Ander's hand flew across his notebook as he tried to keep up.

"That's Bob Simmons. He's a councilman. Pat Thomas. She's the chair of the school board. Kagiso Maharaj. He's a very important venture capitalist who invests in everything. They all live in Kentwood."

Ander turned the page in his notebook. "Kentwood? Good. That place is already a fortress. Chief Gray flooded it with deputies."

Amy gave a bark of humorless laughter. "Has she? Well, I hope they're more alert than she is."

"What do you mean?"

Amy tapped the screen. "Back row, second seat on the left. That's Chief Gray."

## 35

Kentwood Police Chief Jean Gray sipped her coffee and scrolled down the budget spreadsheet.

*This is business as usual. This is what I'm supposed to be doing. Not dealing with psychos.*

Few people understood how much time she spent staring at a screen, planning budgets, and allocating funds. Whenever she met people at events, they assumed she spent her day running around Kentwood collaring bad guys.

She had officers for the hands-on work. She was a manager. A C-level executive of crime fighting. And the CEOs she knew didn't spend *their* days on the factory floor. Hell, they probably didn't even know where the factory floor was.

They were leaders, like her.

Her job was to set strategy, to point the ship in the right direction. Her people were responsible for lowering sails and swabbing the decks. The captain belonged at the helm, not belowdecks.

And it was also her job to make sure the department had all the resources it needed.

If Kentwood wanted its police department to be the best in the country, to have the latest communications gear, the most sustainable office building, and the most powerful electric cars, they needed the richest residents to write the biggest checks.

Jean had always been good at persuading the town's wealthiest residents to do exactly that. City Council would never find another fundraiser like her.

She knew some people whispered about the hours she spent hobnobbing with Kentwood's rich and successful. But she didn't go to those parties, concerts, and weddings because she wanted to. She sipped champagne and ate *vol-au-vents* because those people paid for her city's protection.

For example, on the very night of Jeremy Deem's murder, she'd cemented a hundred-thousand-dollar donation from a property developer at the children's recital.

*One hundred grand for a single evening of mediocre music.*

That was her job. Fundraiser came first, followed by cop, administrator, and frontline general.

Jean dropped her cursor on a line estimating office renovations. She'd allocated two hundred and thirty grand to improve the rec room and rebuild the canteen. Her officers would have a barista-quality coffee machine, a pool table, and a pizza oven. Her people deserved nothing but the best.

But promised funds weren't the same as delivered funds. If these murders continued, no money would come anywhere near the department's coffers. Kentwood's well-heeled weren't going to buy the police department a pizza oven when they worried about having their throats garroted.

"Dammit!"

She highlighted the renovation funds in yellow. The rec room and canteen were now on the chopping block.

These killings needed to be stopped. If wallets stayed closed, she'd have to start cutting hours too. First to go would be overtime. Then maybe a couple of officers would have to go part-time.

She rubbed her temples.

*A few more dead families and the city council might find someone to replace* me.

The FBI didn't seem to be helping too much.

Most people thought she'd brought the Feds onto the case to provide needed assistance. That was true to some extent. In reality, though, she'd brought them in so they would pocket the enormous cost of the forensic investigation.

But seriously? They should have done better.

Damn Paul Slade. He'd been all calm authority and reassurances. But so far, he hadn't done a damn thing. The killer was still out there.

If she hadn't pulled every officer she could spare into the wealthier neighborhoods and encouraged people to pay for their own security, she'd probably be scraping even more brains off living room floors and piano keyboards by now.

*What a waste of time. And who's going to pay for the FBI's failure? I am.*

She sighed.

Someone knocked on her office door.

Chief Gray minimized the spreadsheet window.

*No need to let everyone know their overtime and hours are at risk.*

"Yes?"

An officer poked his head around the door. Benny was a good kid. He'd only been with the department for ten months. If the donations stopped and the cuts started, he'd be one of the first to go.

"What can I do for you, Benny?"

He scratched the top of his head. "We've got an incident, Chief."

"An *incident*?" The young officer had a bad habit of

dancing around sticky subjects. She had no time. "What's happening? Exactly."

Benny held the door open. "Well, it's down at the music store."

Jean took a deep breath. "*What* is down at the music store?"

"Someone's gone and taken some hostages."

Unable to believe she'd heard him correctly, she shook her head. "What?" A lunatic with a gun and a store full of people. That was all she needed right now. "Hostages? Who's holding hostages? How many?"

Benny shrugged, making him appear around twelve years old. "Don't rightly know, Chief. Report just came in. But there's one thing that's strange."

"Just one? What else is strange, other than someone holding hostages in the music store?"

"Well, Chief, thing is, the hostage-taker kidnapper person…he's demanding *you* come down there."

A shudder passed through Jean. The television feeds would be busy tonight.

*Shit.*

"Me? Definitely me?"

"Says he wants Chief Jean Gray. He asked for you by name. And he says if you don't get there in the next ten minutes, he's going to shoot a hostage."

She didn't understand. For a moment, she sat there at her desk, her mouth turning dry as she processed through various possibilities.

Was this a joke?

Had an ex gone crazy and decided today was the day for some sort of revenge?

No. None of that made sense.

*Shit.*

Music store. Pianos. Dead people. Guns. Bunny suit.

*Shit. Shit. Shit.*

Benny licked his lips. "Chief?"

She could just say no, couldn't she? Or...she could march straight down there, figure out what was going on, and save the day.

All the national news stations would seek to have her on their morning news shows. Her name would stretch across every newspaper from coast to coast.

Jean reached for her hat. "All right. I'm on my way. Tell the FBI to meet me there."

## 36

I began at the beginning, following the sage advice of Lewis Carroll's king.

*"Begin at the beginning...and go on till you come to the end: then stop."*

Chopin's Piano Concerto no. 1. Such a beautiful piece. I planned to play all three movements with tremendous care, giving due respect to the composer. When I reached the end of the first movement, I would stop. Then I'd play the second section from the beginning.

The chief should be here by then.

If she wasn't, I'd make my audience one listener smaller.

But she'd come. I was sure she would. And once she was here, I'd move on to Bach and play through all his seven concertos. Sure, Bach wrote those for a harpsichord, but this piano was warm and lively. The chief would enjoy listening.

The chief and the rest of my audience.

They sat lined up on the floor before me. One of the obnoxious youths sat curled up, sweat running down his temple. Not finding me so funny now, I imagined. He closed his eyes and trembled.

"Don't sleep! Don't you dare sleep."

The boy opened his eyes, fear darkening their youthful vigor.

Neither of the teenagers had left the store by the time I'd returned from the car, my gun in one pocket and the piano wire curled in the other. The store assistant was there, too, of course, and the guitar-strap-buying guy.

How unfortunate for them.

I'd only wanted to eliminate the people who'd disrespected my concert. Those people had openly mocked music. They had to be stopped. With them gone, genuine aficionados could assume their leadership roles. And true music could receive the dignity it deserved.

Who knew such people were everywhere?

No one in the store had tried to be a hero when I came back inside. They laughed when they saw my mask, but not for long. They stopped their guffaws fast enough when I pulled out my gun. I didn't have any rope, but I'd always been an excellent improviser—just ask my jazz professor.

Guitar straps served as adequate substitutes. The guitarist sobbed when the store assistant tied his hands behind his back. His tears soaked his beard, and snot darkened his mustache. I felt sorry for him. Of all the young men in the lineup, he probably loved music the most.

So what harm was I doing him? He was about to be privy to a private concert. He would hear the classics. Definitely Chopin and Bach and perhaps even Beethoven, if we had the time.

I allowed the guitarist to make the call to the cops. He'd expressed my demands well.

Chief Gray would be here soon. She would be my last, most likely.

A law enforcement officer. A person who should have shown respect.

The chief had failed on so many levels. First, she failed me, and now, she hadn't protected her residents.

I doubted I would make it out of this store a free man, but I would play for her one more time. And when I was done, I'd let her sleep forever.

They'd come for me, but the worst would be over. I'd removed the most egregious offenders.

Lisa would be free to play in a world appreciative of her talents.

As she deserved. My little girl was so gifted.

When I reached the end of Chopin, I began Bach at the beginning.

## 37

Hagen hadn't bothered with the Explorer. Instead, he and Chloe had jumped in his Corvette, and he almost smiled as it screamed to a halt a block away from G-Clef Instruments. Skid marks probably burned the asphalt. Burnt rubber scorched his nostrils.

"Nice driving, Evel Knievel." Chloe rubbed her chest where the seat belt had engaged.

*Oops.*

"Did it hurt your shoulder?"

Raising her chin, Chloe narrowed her blue eyes. "Of course not."

Not that she'd ever admit to being anything close to human.

Hagen was already out of the 'Vette and taking in the scene by the time Stella and Ander pulled in behind them.

Half a dozen law enforcement vehicles blocked the road ahead. Their angled, haphazard parking was a clear sign something was horribly wrong.

Behind the police cruisers, officers crouched with rifles and pistols aimed at the music store fifty yards up the road. A similar line of officers blocked the road on the other side of the store.

In the space between the deputies' cars and the evacuated stores, a strange and uncomfortable calm had fallen.

No one walked down the sidewalk or sat on the green benches surrounding the front planter. The shuttered furniture boutique, the toy store, and the ice cream parlor next to the music store were all empty. Although the doors of the stores stood open, no one passed in or out. There was no traffic.

The music store itself was unlit. Either Boris Kerne had turned out the lights, or the chief's men had cut the power in hopes of driving him out sooner. The music store was flanked by the ice cream parlor and a sandwich shop, so there were no side windows. A guitar display dominated the front window, but it was a walled-in display. There were no other windows.

"We're blind."

From down the street came the muffled, distant sound of piano music.

Chloe pulled her blue jacket with FBI emblazoned across the back in yellow letters over her Kevlar vest. "This is our stop. Unless you plan to stand here and watch."

Hagen tightened the Velcro on his own vest. "Maybe stand here and listen. As long as he's playing, we know he's not killing."

Chloe started toward Ander and Stella. "True. But he won't play forever."

Hagen joined her, pulling on his own jacket.

Slade's black SUV pulled up.

Their boss slammed his door and was halfway across the road before Ander and Stella had finished climbing out of their vehicle.

"Status?"

"Just got here." Hagen zipped his jacket.

Slade turned toward the line of cars and caught the eye of an officer.

The young man came running when Slade waved him over. Traces of acne decorated the officer's forehead beneath his wide-brimmed hat.

Slade waited for him to draw near. "What's your name, son?"

"I'm Benny. Er...Officer Benjamin Neves, sir."

"What's the status here? Where's Chief Gray? I was told she was on her way."

Benny shuffled his feet. "Oh yeah. She told me to call you."

"Where is she?" Slade's voice was slow and even. Hagen recognized his tone and took a step back. It often came right before Slade exploded. "Why am I talking to you and not her? Why isn't she here?"

"Oh, she's here, sir."

Slade's eyes closed and reopened on a long exhale. The kid probably didn't deserve the blast Slade would give him if he didn't get to the point soon. Chief Gray really should have trained him better.

Slade's voice dropped another octave. "Then why can't I see her here, Officer?"

Benny nodded in the direction of the music store. "Because she's in there, sir. Went in about five minutes ago."

*What the hell?*

Hagen blinked and peered over Benny's shoulder. There was nothing to learn from the music store façade, though. Luckily, the piano music continued.

Slade ran a hand over his face. "Are you saying she went into the music store?"

Benny gave a deep nod. "Yes, sir."

"What the hell does she think she's doing in there? Who the hell authorized that?"

"I-I…" Benny spluttered, his face turning neon red. "I…erm."

Hagen grabbed Benny's shoulders and spun him around. "Officer, listen to me. I want you to tell me exactly what happened before your boss walked straight into a hostage situation."

Benny swallowed hard. He adjusted his hat and cleared his throat.

"Officer, now!"

"Right, yes. Sorry. He…the guy inside…he released one of the hostages. A young guy. He came out and said if Chief Gray came into the store, the guy at the piano would release everyone else."

Hagen glanced at Slade. His boss's face was like granite. Hagen assumed the SSA and everyone else was thinking what he was—Chief Gray was either incredibly brave or incredibly stupid.

And possibly both.

"After she went in, did Boris Kerne release everyone else?"

The officer's eyes widened, confused. "Boris…?"

"Kerne. The guy at the piano. And I'm guessing he has a gun, too, right? And a length of piano wire?"

"Yeah. That's what the hostage said. How did you—?"

"Did he release the hostages when Chief Gray went in?"

"Er…no. No, he didn't."

*Stupid, then. Chief Gray had been incredibly stupid.*

Benny removed his hat. He rubbed his sweaty blond hair and rammed his hat back on again. "But we didn't really expect him to release them."

Chloe stepped closer to the line of cars, her hands in the pockets of her FBI jacket. "No, I should think not."

"No. I mean, he didn't say he'd release them *now*."

Hagen looked to the heavens, took in the clear, blue sky, then lowered his gaze and stared into Benny's face. "You know, Officer. You need to spit out everything you know. Otherwise, we're going send you in there to replace the hostages yourself."

Benny swallowed hard. "Yes, yes. Sorry. He said if Chief Gray came in, he'd release the hostages, but only after he finished his performance."

Slade swore quietly. He strode back to his car, returning with a pair of binoculars. Hagen and the rest of the team followed him to the line of cars in front of the music store. Slade rested his elbows on the roof of a police vehicle and peered through the lenses.

After a minute, he passed the glasses to Hagen.

"I can only see one entrance. There's probably another around back." Slade turned to Chloe. "Go find out about the back layout from one of the other store managers. Maybe there's an entrance that isn't apparent from a visual. Quick."

Chloe double-timed it to a cluster of lookie-loos wearing ice cream parlor uniforms.

"Ander, go get the hostage who was released. We need info, now."

Ander took off down the street.

Hagen lifted the binoculars to his eyes and adjusted the focus.

Not that it mattered. The most he could distinguish was the store logo on the front entrance. While the door itself was glass, the door was covered with notices of upcoming concerts, gigs, and musical tutoring. There wasn't a spare inch of space from top to bottom.

"Here's the released hostage." Ander led a skinny young man in hipster jeans and a Pink Floyd t-shirt forward. He was still trembling. "Gideon Harrison. Twenty years old from Brentwood."

"It's all right. You're safe." Slade laid a surprisingly gentle hand on the young man's shoulder. "We need your help. We need to know what happened. We also need to know the interior of the store. How many people are in there right now?"

"Four. It was my buddy and me, and then some guy who works for the store and another guy. The psycho let me go, and I told the police chief what he'd said. That's when she went inside."

Hagen took notes as the young man described the layout of the room, including the location of the piano, where the hostages were tied up, and how they were secured.

"The guy's nuts. All my buddy did was ask if he was the guy in this funny video who—"

"The video with everyone sleeping?" Stella stepped forward, already showing the hostage the footage.

"That's the one. He freakin' lost it, man. He left and went to his car. It was funny, you know, so my buddy and I watched him from the store."

"Which vehicle?"

He pointed to a beat-up Maxima. "He got on his phone, and we stopped watching. Figured he'd drive off after that. Then he came back in...with a gun. Said he was tying us all up and would kill whoever yawned or fell asleep while he played." The kid shook his head, making his shaggy hair wave and wobble. "It was like torture. He's good but *slow*, you know?"

Distantly, a piano poured out notes, and Hagen knew the tempo was far too slow. He understood what the kid meant about torture.

Chloe jogged back. "I got a diagram from the parlor owner. He says there's a back passage that connects all the stores. He knows the rear door to the music shop opens into a small storage area, which leads to the office, which *then* gets you into the main store floor."

Slade's phone rang. He answered, listened, and nodded. "Affirmative." He hung up and turned to his team. "Put all this information together. SWAT is two minutes away. Earpieces. Phone connection to me."

A phone connection meant communication would only be one-way. Slade could communicate the outside world to them. They'd recon and then join back up to debrief SWAT. Hagen barely managed to get his earpiece in and connected when the music stopped.

Everyone froze.

*Play, please play*, Hagen willed Boris.

*BANG!*

The gunshot rang out down the street, louder than any piano concerto. Screams sounded inside the store.

Hagen darted forward, but Slade grabbed his upper arm in a vice grip. "Do *not* breach. We need more information, or we'll lose everyone. Hagen, Stella, take the back, see if you can find a good entrance for the SWAT team. Ander, Chloe, to the front, see if there are gaps between those damn flyers. Go!"

## 38

Stella ran behind Hagen as they slipped along the edge of the strip mall, weapons in hand. Together, they turned the corner and followed the rear of the building. A door reading *Deliveries Only* greeted them.

"This is it." Stella turned the handle and was surprised when it opened. She didn't waste time wondering why the mall didn't lock up during business hours. Instead, she led the way inside.

A long, concrete hallway stretched the length of the building, like the ice cream parlor owner had said. Sweat prickled on the back of Stella's neck. Once inside, the temperature dropped about ten degrees, and Stella was suddenly grateful for her jacket.

She stepped left, verifying the first entrance was the ice cream parlor's rear entrance. Someone had drawn an ice cream cone in permanent marker and written *No bigger licks in town* over the metal door.

Hagen stepped to the right, taking the lead.

Stella crept on, following Hagen and moving as quickly

and quietly as she could. Mentally, she noted the layout so she could explain it to the SWAT team.

The piano playing started again, the notes drifting through the empty hallway. Stella breathed out slowly, relieved. Boris the Boringest must have calmed down.

As long as she could hear the notes, she knew what he was doing. They had to get inside before the music stopped.

The store's rear entrance was less than five yards away now. The music grew louder as they approached. Stella wished she knew the piece so she could estimate the amount of time they had before he finished.

And reached for his gun again.

For Chief Gray, Stella knew Boris planned to use the coil of piano wire.

The thought made her shudder. She couldn't let Kerne garrote Chief Gray. They had to stop him. They had to do it together. If she wasn't already shot in the head.

Hagen reached the door. He lifted a hand, his fingers folded into a fist. Stella stopped. They'd reached a metal door identical to the ice cream parlor's—minus the licks comment. Somehow, the music store remained free of graffiti.

They entered the storage room. Shelves, mostly empty, lined the walls. Black instrument cases were stacked neatly. Cardboard boxes labeled *Sheet Music* dominated one entire shelf. Replacement parts were kept in tidy plastic drawers.

"Clear." Hagen's voice was barely audible.

"SWAT's delayed," Slade said into her ear. Hagen paused in front of her, listening. "Use your best judgment."

Stella met Hagen's gaze. He nodded. They understood one another. If they saw an opportunity to end this, they'd take it.

The music was louder here. They were getting very close to their target. Together, matching footstep for footstep, they moved to the next door. According to the parlor owner, it would open to an office, which would open to the sales floor.

Hagen pressed his flat hand down, which meant "stay low." They didn't know if the office had a window or if it was somehow exposed to the pianist. Stella squatted as Hagen opened the door.

The office didn't have a window. A cluttered desk stood to their right. Sticky notes with messages like *Steve needs Monday off* and *Lily's vacay 7$^{th}$–13$^{th}$* sprouted around the computer monitor. A guitar needing strings sat propped against the wall.

Clearing the space, they remained low until they reached the open door. Hagen took the right, while Stella covered the left.

She had the lucky side.

Raising her fingers to her eyes, she indicated to Hagen that she had their suspect in her sight. Well, part of him.

The angle of the piano hid Boris Kerne's face, but she could see his legs working the pedals. The sound grew louder, and Stella was sure the finger work was faster too. Even to her untrained ear, the piece seemed to be reaching a climax.

She pointed at herself and then at the door, communicating her intention to lead.

Hagen raised his hand, signaling, "I don't understand." It was a bullshit response. A flash of anger jolted through her, but before she could repeat her signal, he pointed at his face.

*Oh, no, you don't...*

Stella clamped her mouth shut and lifted her fingers to her eyes again. To punctuate her communication, she mouthed, "Trust me."

*Dammit, stop being such a hero. I can see him.*

Hagen's eyes locked onto hers. His irises were a green so dark they were almost brown. He didn't move. She couldn't read his thoughts, but she could see they were like the piano notes—coming quickly.

She mouthed the words again. "Trust me."

Hagen licked his lips and, after what felt like minutes, gave the "okay" sign.

Stella tightened her grip on her weapon, prepared to go in low and fast.

The music stopped.

Before she could move in, Hagen rushed ahead of her.

There was no adjustment in his stance or shift in his line of vision. One moment he was crouching in front of her, his weapon pointing at the ground. The next, he was diving shoulder-first through the door.

*Damn you, Hagen!*

Stella leapt forward.

Hagen was already a yard ahead of her, his head low, his weapon at the ready. "FBI!" His command voice filled the empty space like a bullet.

Flying through the door, Stella twisted her body and took in the rest of the room. The hostages were lined up on the floor near the piano. As one, they crouched as low as they could, terror more evident in their silence than if they were screaming.

At the piano, Boris Kerne, wearing a morning coat and a rabbit mask, hit one last killer note before lifting his hands from the keys. He half stood between his stool and keyboard.

A gun was in his hand. Aimed at Hagen.

Hagen fired. *Click.*

No bullet in the chamber.

"Nooo!"

Firing off a shot of her own, Stella threw her weight to the side. Her shoulder smashed into Hagen's ribs, knocking him off balance. The edge of the piano exploded, spraying Stella with splinters of black and tan wood.

*Boom.*

A flash burst through the store. She was struck in the side as hard as a kick from a horse.

"Shit!"

Her initial momentum still carrying her sideways, Stella hit a stack of speakers. She tried to brace herself, but her wrist bent—too far backward. Boxes skidded away, but her already injured side hit the corner of one. Pain exploded across the right half of her body.

She landed next to Hagen, who'd recovered from her push and was already on one knee. He racked the slide and opened fire.

Three definitive blasts echoed through the store.

## 39

Three words. Three words were all Stella had said to Hagen since he'd picked her up from the hospital.

She'd given a sigh and a quiet "yes" to his offer to drive her home.

Then she'd said "yes" when he asked if she was still in pain.

Finally, she'd said "no" when he wondered whether he should turn up the car's air-conditioning.

He got nothing more out of her.

She sat there in the passenger seat, sometimes staring out of the front window, sometimes out the side window.

Her left arm was strapped to a splint until the swelling in her broken wrist was reduced. When Hagen hit a pothole, she winced. The broken rib had to hurt like hell, but she wasn't going to complain.

Her silence wasn't what Hagen had expected as he'd sat in the ER waiting room. He'd expected one of two things. She'd be jubilant that they'd stopped Boris Kerne. After all, the hostages had been safely freed, including Chief Gray. The random shot they'd heard had been Boris shooting a guitar.

Killer Note 237

The case was over.

Or, more likely, she'd be pissed at the way he'd forced her to go about it. He'd mentally braced for the lecture he knew would be directed at him.

For two hours, he'd paced the waiting room, hoping the positive result would override how they'd achieved it.

In the waiting room, a television hanging from the corner of the ceiling broadcast a local news channel. Their colleague, Special Agent Martin Lin, had assumed public relations responsibilities, as he was the only member of the team who would never refuse a chance to talk on camera, and he'd also remained a neutral party in this case.

Martin smiled into the lens as the network reran his original statement. "I'm pleased to announce that, through quick thinking and brave action, the Federal Bureau of Investigation was able to resolve a hostage situation with no victims' lives lost. In my view, the strength of partnerships at the federal, state, and local levels once again demonstrates how teamwork…"

*Blah, blah, blah…*

Hagen would have raised a drink to Martin if he'd been holding anything stronger than a vending machine coffee. Not that Martin deserved it. He'd barely had any input on the case. And yet there he was, taking all the glory.

*In my view*, Martin was full of shit.

As the newscast moved on to the weather, Hagen worried.

The truth was, he'd screwed up.

And he knew it.

The most important thing in any operation was trust. Everyone needed to know their jobs, and they needed to know the job everyone else was doing too. Once weapons were drawn, there was no room for doing your own thing and hoping others followed along.

And yet, he'd agreed for Stella to enter the scene first. And then he'd leapt ahead of her.

She hadn't been ready.

Yes, they'd taken out Boris Kerne. Once the mad bunny got his single shot off, Hagen planted his shots into the killer's chest, perforating his morning coat and spraying blood all over his stupid yet terrifying mask.

But if Stella had known what he was going to do, they would have moved together, acting as one. They would have separated to confuse the suspect, forcing him to choose which agent to target.

He'd acted on impulse. Somehow, in the moment, he couldn't let Stella take point. It was the most dangerous position. Before he even knew what he was doing, he was moving, pushing through the door. And, dammit, he still couldn't believe he hadn't chambered a round. He'd never made that mistake before.

If he'd waited, trusted Stella, Boris Kerne might never have fired his weapon.

And Stella wouldn't have had to push Hagen out of the way, taking the bullet herself.

The fact that the bullet hit Stella, slamming like a sledgehammer into her vest, sent a wave of nausea through him. He was lucky it hadn't killed her.

What he'd done had broken something beyond rib cages, and he needed to repair it.

"I guess you'll be getting a cast for that wrist in a couple of days." He kept his eyes on the road, trying to be responsible. He couldn't bear the silence anymore. "Happened to me when I was a kid. Must've been about sixteen. Went up for a dunk, got body checked, and came down like a sack of potatoes. Had the cast on for about six weeks. Got out of all kinds of nasty homework."

Stella stared out the window.

Hagen swallowed.

"Just think, if the stereo stack had been a little farther away, your wrist would have been fine too."

Her jaw slid from side to side, but her mouth didn't open.

They drove on. Traffic built up as they headed onto Route 41.

"Hitting rush hour. This could take a while now, especially at this junction."

Still, Stella didn't answer.

"Hey, did you hear?" He was babbling like an idiot. He was an idiot. "Dani's replacement, while she's on maternity leave, will be here tomorrow. Stacy Lark. Ex-cop. Should make Ander happy, having another woman around the team."

His laugh sounded strange to his ears, and by the time he snapped his mouth shut, Stella was staring at him.

He fell silent. It was physically painful for him.

"Who had he been talking to?"

Hagen did a double take at the unexpected question. "What?"

"Boris. That kid, Gideon, said that Boris left the music store and went to his car. He called someone. Who did he call?"

Hagen shook his head. "I don't know. The CSU will probably trace it to a burner, and we'll never find out."

Stella twisted the gold stud in her ear. "Aren't you curious?"

"Of course, but until the techs sweep Boris's vehicle and that hotel room, curious is about as far as it goes."

Silence descended between them once again. Hagen was surprised when Stella was the first to break it.

"Tell me something."

*Finally.*

"Sure, anything."

"Can I trust you?"

The question was a gut punch. "Can you...? Of course you can trust me."

"Do you trust me?"

He didn't hesitate. "Absolutely."

"Really? Because I asked you to trust me at that door. I knew where Kerne was. I could see him from my position. You couldn't. I asked you to trust me, and you told me you would. You didn't."

"Stella, I—"

"What the hell were you thinking? Did you think I couldn't handle it? Dammit, Hagen!"

She slammed a fist onto the car's dashboard, a move that made Hagen flinch. And not because she might dent it.

"I'm sorry, I just—"

"Just what? You *just* did whatever the hell you wanted, didn't you?"

"I wanted the hostages freed. That was all." It sounded weak, even to him.

"So did I!" She raised her fist again, but this time dropped it into her lap. "That's what we all wanted. And we wanted to do it in the safest way possible, minimizing risks and working together. You can't act on the first stupid impulse that enters your damn brain. You're not judge, jury, and executioner here! We bring them in. Alive, if we can. That's the job."

Hagen's cheeks grew hot. A space opened in the lane next to him, and he steered into it, hitting the gas, then slammed the brakes before almost colliding with the car in front. He'd gained about ten yards and sent Stella into her seat belt, forcing another wince from her.

"And can you drive more carefully, dammit?"

It was his turn to be silent. He drummed his fingers on the steering wheel and waited for the traffic to move.

Stella was right.

He knew she was right.

Hagen took a deep breath. "I screwed up. I let the moment get the better of me, and I...I got it wrong. I'll do better."

Stella relaxed beside him. The apology seemed to have shifted something. Maybe he should have started with sorry. Sometimes that was all someone needed to hear.

"Hagen, it's not only this case. I'm going to go back to Atlanta. I'm going to face Joel, and I'm going to get him to tell me what he knows. I'd like to have someone with me. But if I can't trust you...if I can't..." She stopped and took a deep breath. "Look, I told Ander what I'm doing. If I can't trust you to support me when I need you to, I'll bring him."

A chill passed over Hagen.

Fear, panic, anger, jealousy. They were all there, roiling around inside of him, igniting in his chest.

He slowed his breathing.

*Stay calm. She's not taking Ander. She won't. You've got this.*

"You need me with you in Atlanta, not Ander."

*You shouldn't have even told Ander. This is none of his damn business. Let Ander deal with rebuilding his family and settling into a happy life with a house and kids and blah, blah, blah. That's all he ever wanted. You and me? We've got more important things to do.*

Stella spoke quietly. "I need someone I can trust. Someone who tells me the truth."

The SUV in front of them rolled forward a yard and then stopped. Hagen followed, then pulled on the hand brake and put the gear into park. He wasn't going to leave this spot until he said his piece.

Turning in his seat, Hagen looked her in the eye. "You want the truth? All right. Here it is. I was interested in your search for your father's killer because I figured it would take me to my father's killer. It's the same guy. Has to be. My dad used to tell me that one man controlled Memphis back then. He had his finger in everything. No one would've killed a cop like your dad and a lawyer like mine without his say-so. I thought you could lead me to him."

Stella's cold expression didn't change. "You used me."

"No, I…"

The blockage had cleared. The lanes on each side of the car started to flow. Behind the Corvette came blasts of repeated honking, then the squeal of tires as the cars pulled into the neighboring lanes.

Hagen still didn't move.

"Yeah. Maybe. At first. I didn't know you then. But I've been hunting down the man who shot my dad since the *day* he died. There's barely a day I haven't thought about what I'll do to him when I catch him. And then you come along and, in an instant, *boom*, a lead. The first real lead I've ever had."

A car drove past, the driver screaming out of the open window. "Get out of the damn road!"

"And now?"

"Now it's different. I still want to find whoever killed our dads. But I want to do it for you as well. I want to do it *with* you, and I think we'll find him faster if we work together." A series of loud horn blasts sounded. Hagen kept his eyes on Stella. "We have the same goal. Exactly the same goal. You can trust me."

The long, searching glance Stella gave him left Hagen feeling exposed. But he didn't move. He would do nothing to give her a reason not to believe him. He didn't look away.

Stella blinked. "All right. But we bring in everyone. It's time. This person has murdered at least two people. We're running up against witness protection. We need help. I've learned that. You should learn it too. Anyway, Mac and Ander already know, so let's put everyone to work."

Hagen took a deep breath. That wasn't what he'd planned. This thing was already getting too big. Another horn sounded behind him.

"Okay."

He released the hand brake and put the car into drive.

## 40

Sis hit the play button on her phone. The video was slightly crooked. The lens was angled, and its wideness stretched the room, so the end of Stella's bed curved, walleyed, at the corners.

Sis gave a small, satisfied grin. The camera was working. And Stella hadn't spotted it.

FBI, man. Sometimes they could be so dumb.

Sis dropped her feet onto the upturned milk crate behind her trailer and propped her phone against a bottle of Jack Daniel's. She lifted her glass. Ice would have been good. Jack should always have ice. But her trailer didn't have a freezer, and even the small refrigerator barely kept food much lower than room temperature.

She'd gotten lucky with this trailer, though. Hers was the last in the park, with a view of the pasture during the daytime. Now, at night, with the moon overhead, she could watch the shadow of the trees in the silvery moonlight and enjoy some privacy.

Better. Sometimes this work really had its moments.

*"And now, back to our regularly scheduled programming."*

On the right of the screen, the bathroom door opened, and Stella emerged, drying her hair with a towel. Her pink shorts barely covered the tops of her thighs. Her camisole top revealed an expanse of flat tummy and the bottom of a bandage that wrapped around her midriff. Bruises covered her otherwise golden skin. When Stella tossed the towel on the back of a chair, Sis saw her arm was in a splint.

She bent closer to the screen. "Aw, did you have a hard day at work today, Stella? Guess stopping that loon wasn't as easy as your friend on the TV made it out to be. Shame the crazy bunny didn't try a little harder. Would have made all our lives easier."

Stella ran a hand over her ribs and climbed into bed. Her arm reached over the top of the lens hidden in her bedside clock. The room turned dark.

Sis leaned back in her chair. On the screen, silver moonlight merged with the orange glow of streetlights shining through the apartment window. Sis could make out Stella's shape under the bedclothes. She was already asleep.

Poor thing. The case must have really taken a toll on her.

Sis aimed an imaginary gun and pointed it at the screen. She pulled the invisible trigger.

"Bang. Bang. Too easy."

Her phone vibrated. Sis stopped the video and took the call.

"Looks like your little friend has been busy." The Officer's voice was low and deep and straight to the point.

"Not now, she's not. She's sleeping like a baby. I was just watching her."

"Hm. Good. I saw the news."

"Yeah, we almost got lucky. But fortune favors the bold...I can make us lucky myself. She's like a baby bird with a broken wing right now. Be almost a mercy to put her out of her misery."

"Is she miserable, Sam?"

Sis hesitated. Whenever The Officer called her by her real name, she started. It made her feel as if she were getting called into the principal's office.

"Out of my misery, then. C'mon. What are we beating about the bush for? Let's wipe out this problem now. You know what she wants. You know what she's looking for. Let's deal with it now."

Silence.

Was he thinking? Deciding?

Or pushing down his anger because he was in a place where he couldn't raise his voice?

There was no sound in the background, so Sis couldn't tell if he was in a public area.

She waited. The Officer returned with a chuckle, low and guttural. "You're always so enthusiastic. That's what I love about you. But hold off. We don't want to draw attention to ourselves unless we absolutely have to. She's still a way off, and we need to know who else she's involved. Let's see what she knows and who's helping her."

The phone went dead.

"Goodnight to you too."

Sis propped it back up against the bottle, hit the play button again, and slugged down the rest of her Jack. On the screen, Stella slept contentedly.

"You're this close, Stella Knox." Sis held her index finger and thumb an inch apart. "This close to joining your father."

## 41

The next several days were paperwork heavy, and Stella gained a new appreciation for what Chloe had gone through while recovering from her gunshot wound. Typing one-handed was no picnic.

Hagen had been put on administrative leave while the officer-involved shooting investigation was conducted. Since Boris had taken a shot at them, Hagen was cleared in only a few days.

During that time, Mac's bruises had faded while Dani and her little family bonded at home. After minimal downtime, Stella had been tasked with going through hours and hours of video footage. It was one of her least favorite tasks but involved little use of her hand.

After the crime scene techs had finished going through Boris Kerne's vehicle and motel room, they'd found a small digital video camera the musician used an average of four to eight hours each day.

From writing music to conducting a pretend orchestra, Boris had filmed himself for reasons Stella could only speculate. Maybe he was lonely, and the camera gave him the audience he desperately sought. Maybe he'd used the footage to criticize himself as harshly as he'd been criticized by others.

It was sad, really.

She would have begged for a different assignment if one question hadn't continued to nag at her...

Who'd been on that phone with him outside the music store?

It was driving her crazy, but maybe tech would have answers for her soon.

She was well into her third hour of watching Boris inside his motel room when a *bam-bam-bam* nearly caused her to drop her cup of cocoa. Boris had been lying on his motel bed, conducting some unseen symphony when the banging started. A framed print above the bed fell, nearly landing on the man's head—though his reflexes were quick enough to save him from injury.

*"Will you turn that crap down?"*

Stella sat straighter, pressing the headphones against her ears so she could better understand what was happening on the screen. From what she could gather, the occupant of the next room wasn't happy with Boris's musical selection and wasn't afraid to make that fact known.

*"You wouldn't recognize genius if Mozart played your entrails like a harp,"* Boris said to the complainer, though not loud enough for the words to carry through the wall.

He tossed the fallen artwork across the room and, still muttering something she couldn't quite catch, turned the volume down. When all was quiet again, Boris put his head back on the pillow, his hands back to the task of mimicking a conductor.

Stella sighed and reached for her mouse, ready to fast-forward through the footage when a familiar vibration interrupted the music. On the monitor, Boris sat up and reached for a phone. Instead of raising the device to his ear, he tapped the screen.

"Yes."

"Brava, Boris, brava."

As she watched, the pale man's expression relaxed into the first smile she'd seen. He raised a hand to his heart and appeared genuinely touched by the caller's praise.

*"Your performance last night was masterful. Perfection."*

Stella reached for the volume control, intent on the caller's words. The voice was deep with a mixture of southern genteel and upscale posh. She recognized that voice, but from where?

*"Thank you. I'm glad you're pleased."*

*"I am. You're not done, though."*

Without being told, Boris reached for pen and paper. *"Who's next?"*

*"Donovan Freeman. I have it on good authority that Donovan and his wife, Pamela, engage in movie night most Friday evenings. Gaining access to the home will be easy. You'll simply wait by the gate for the pizza delivery guy, then enter the home immediately afterwards."*

Stella's heart was pounding in her ears so hard she was surprised to hear the rest of the conversation. Address. Times. Even the best place for Boris to park his car was outlined in the call.

*"Do you understand?"*

Where had she heard that voice before?

*"Yes. Thank you."*

*"You're welcome, Boris. Music demands respect. Focus. And, by extension, the musician deserves respect and focus too. To offer anything else is an unforgivable insult...a crime. Crimes must be punished."*

Boris's smile widened, his hand lifting to his heart. *"I'm the punisher."*

*"Yes. You still have work to do."*

*"I do, and I shall."*

As the call ended, Stella stared at the screen, processing everything she'd just discovered.

Boris Kerne was no doubt their killer, but he hadn't worked alone.

She hit replay, focusing hard on the caller's voice.

*"Music demands respect. Focus. And, by extension, the musician deserves respect and focus too."*

Memory came flooding back as she listened a third time. Stella had been standing outside the Deems' home speaking to Jeremy Deem Jr.—Jem—about his dead family.

Stella closed her eyes and replayed the scene. She'd wanted to know why his daughter had been too tired to visit her grandparents after her recital. She remembered how insulted he'd seemed by the question.

"Even for a musician so young, a performance can be taxing. You see, music demands respect. Focus. Had my daughter been filled with youthful energy following the recital, I would have been disappointed in her."

*Music demands respect. Focus.*

That was all it took.

Stella bolted toward Slade's door with the information—and a new scope of the investigation was opened just like that.

By the following day, other SD cards revealed similar recorded conversations.

When they gathered enough evidence to question Jeremy Deem's son officially, it hadn't taken much pressure for Jem to crumble.

His motive? Money. Plain and simple.

The junior Deem was smart enough to know that he'd be

the primary suspect in his parents' murders. But, by manipulating a very sick man into becoming a serial killer, Jem believed he would escape prosecution with his daddy's millions.

He almost did.

Stella was relieved and then furious.

*Nobody should get away with murder.*

And yet, two people that she knew of were... The man who'd killed her father, and the man who'd killed Hagen's.

She picked up her phone and started a group text.

*My place for pizza and beer at six tonight? I need you. Please don't say no.*

※

A few hours later, everyone was in her apartment. Stella had never had so many people in her place at the same time.

Ander and Mac sat on the little sofa under the window. Caleb perched on the sofa's arm. Martin leaned against the window ledge next to him, showing off his wink meme that was still flying around the internet nine days after Boris Kerne's death.

Stella had started to sweat, causing the cast on her arm to itch. The plaster was already covered in the team's scrawled signatures.

Mac had even added a doodle of a full martini glass topped with two olives. Stella wondered how professional that would appear next time she had to grill a witness. Long sleeves for a little while, she supposed.

"Who wants a beer?" Hagen insisted on helping Stella serve her guests.

Five hands went up, including one attached to a broken wrist.

He pulled a six-pack out of the fridge and set it on the kitchen island.

Stella grinned as she took an outstretched bottle from Hagen.

Her studio might have never seemed so small, but it had also never felt so warm.

There was friendship here and support, camaraderie. For the first time, she had the real sense of a team behind her. In whatever she wanted to do. She'd never felt less lonely.

*Hope nothing changes in the next few minutes.*

There was a knock on the door.

"I'll get it."

Hagen lobbed a bottle across the room to Ander, who caught it one-handed. The move drew an eye roll from Stella and a round of applause from Mac.

Chloe was the last to arrive. She took Hagen's open bottle from his hand and stepped past him into the room.

Taking a long slug of what had been Hagen's beer a moment before, Chloe perched on one of the barstools at the counter. "We should do this every time Hagen decides to charge into a hostage situation, guns blazing. Though, frankly, I'm not sure there's enough liquor in this town."

She took another slug of beer.

Stella glanced at Hagen, whose cheeks reddened.

It was time to get down to business. "All right. I know we want to celebrate the end of another difficult case…and Hagen's heroism…and Martin's PR stylings." She lifted her bottle to Martin, who raised his own. "But there's something I need to tell you all before the pizza arrives."

She paused and set her bottle on the kitchen island, words failing her. There was so much she had to explain.

Mac gave her a small, encouraging smile.

A warmth spread through Stella's chest. She could do this.

"I need your help. As many of you know, my dad was a cop. He was murdered in the line of duty. His partner, before his own death, told me the people behind his murder were dirty cops."

Caleb lowered his bottle and rested an arm on his knee. "You serious?"

Stella nodded. "In those days, Memphis was as dirty as…as…"

Chloe leaned forward. "As the bathroom in an East Nasty dive bar?"

"Dirtier."

Chloe made a low whistle. "Glad I've never been to Memphis."

"Anyway, with Mac's help, I've learned my father's partner *didn't* die. He's in witness protection in Atlanta, and…Hagen and I are planning to go down there to confront him and find out what happened to my dad."

Hagen took over. "There's a very good chance the person behind the death of Stella's father was also responsible for my dad's shooting. We want to find him."

Chloe took a long swig of her beer, then turned serious. "I wish you both luck, but why are you telling us? If the two of you—and Mac—want to blow your careers by breaking witness protection protocols, you should be keeping it on the down-low."

"Not this time." Mac pushed to the edge of the sofa. "Someone's been following Stella. We don't know if it's witness protection or one of the bad guys from Memphis, but we all need to keep an eye out. Watch her back."

Chloe nodded. "Yeah. Can't come for one of us without running into all of us." She didn't look at Stella, but her words flowed through Stella like warm honey.

Ander rolled his bottle between his palms. "Maybe we

should bring in Slade. If we all know, then maybe the boss should know too."

Hagen shook his head. "He'll want to bring in the Memphis PD. Dirty cops in their area should be their problem. But I can't see them digging into it, can you?"

The room was silent. A fourteen-year-old case involving corrupt police officers was too easy to file away and ignore.

Chloe shrugged. "All right. So this stuff stays with us for now. Let us know what you need."

Stella could have hugged the badass agent, but there was a decent chance Chloe would never speak to her again if she did.

The moment was broken by Freddie Mercury belting out "We Are The Champions" in Martin's pocket. He put his bottle on the window ledge and pulled out his device. He smiled when he saw the screen.

"My sister. She's in town for the weekend. You guys have got to meet her. She's the best damn lawyer in New York. She just went out to get some wine for us." He glanced around the room. "Hey, you rednecks think *I* talk funny? You listen to her. She's been living in Queens for the last three years. Sounds like she joined the Goodfellas."

He laughed and turned his phone on speaker.

"Hey, Jane!"

"Is this Martin Lin?" The caller didn't have a New York accent. It was a woman's voice, but southern and hoarse, as though it had been stretched and torn from hours of screaming.

Martin frowned at his phone. "Uh-huh. Who's this? Where's Jane?"

"Who?"

Martin stiffened, appearing ready to leap through the device and beat the woman on the other side. "My sister. Get my sister on the phone."

"Your sister?" Her laugh bordered on evil. "Oh, honey, you're never going to see your sister again."

*The End*
*To be continued...*

Thank you for reading.
All of the *Stella Knox Series* books can be found on Amazon.

# ACKNOWLEDGMENTS

How does one properly thank everyone involved in taking a dream and making it a reality? Here goes.

In addition to our families, whose unending support provided the foundation for us to find the time and energy to put these thoughts on paper, we want to thank the editors who polished our words and made them shine.

Many thanks to our publisher for risking taking on two newbies and giving us the confidence to become bona fide authors.

More than anyone, we want to thank you, our readers, for sharing your most important asset, your time, with this book. We hope with all our hearts we made it worthwhile.

Much love,
*Mary & Stacy*

# ABOUT THE AUTHOR

**Mary Stone**

Mary Stone lives among the majestic Blue Ridge Mountains of East Tennessee with her two dogs, four cats, a couple of energetic boys, and a very patient husband.

As a young girl, she would go to bed every night, wondering what type of creature might be lurking underneath. It wasn't until she was older that she learned that the creatures she needed to most fear were human.

Today, she creates vivid stories with courageous, strong heroines and dastardly villains. She invites you to enter her world of serial killers, FBI agents but never damsels in distress. Her female characters can handle themselves, going toe-to-toe with any male character, protagonist or antagonist.

Discover more about Mary Stone on her website.
www.authormarystone.com

**Stacy O'Hare**

Growing up in West Virginia, most of the women in Stacy O'Hare's family worked in the medical field. Stacy was no exception and followed in their footsteps, becoming a nurse's aid. It wasn't until she had a comatose patient she became attached to and made up a whole life story about—with a past as an FBI agent included—that she discovered her love of stories. She started jotting them down, and typing them out, and expanding them when she got off shift. Somehow, they turned into a book. Then another. Now, she's over the moon to be releasing her first series.

Connect with Mary Online

- facebook.com/authormarystone
- goodreads.com/AuthorMaryStone
- bookbub.com/profile/3378576590
- pinterest.com/MaryStoneAuthor